"I don't know how to act with you. What are we supposed to do?" Holly asked her protector.

Jack's gray eyes sparkled as he grinned. Her heart fluttered. The transformation was amazing. His whole face lit up and his harsh features turned devastatingly handsome. She tried to focus on what he was saying.

"We're supposed to be married. So act like a newly-wed. Oh, by the way. I put my stuff in the guest room, but I'll be sleeping with you," Jack said.

"You'll what?" Holly croaked.

"We can't take the chance that your stalker might see anything that would tell him we aren't sleeping together. We're pretty sure he has access to your house. So everything must point to a happy newly-wed couple. You have a king-size bed, don't you?"

Holly nodded slowly. She felt paralyzed in place. A vision of Jack in her bed, tangled in her sheets rose before her eyes. She realized she was still nodding, and stopped.

"Don't worry," he said. "I'll stay on my side of the bed. I'm an honorable man...."

Dear Harlequin Intrigue Reader,

Take a very well-deserved break from Thanksgiving preparations and rejuvenate yourself with Harlequin Intrigue's tempting offerings this month!

To start off the festivities, Harper Allen brings you *Covert Cowboy*—the next riveting installment of COLORADO CONFIDENTIAL. Watch the sparks fly when a Native American secret agent teams up with the headstrong mother of his unborn child to catch a slippery criminal. Looking to live on the edge? Then enter the dark and somber HEARTSKEEP estate—with caution!—when Dani Sinclair brings you *The Second Sister*—the next book in her gothic trilogy.

The thrills don't stop there! *His Mysterious Ways* pairs a ruthless mercenary with a secretive seductress as they ward off evil forces. Don't miss this new series in Amanda Stevens's extraordinary QUANTUM MEN books. Join Mallory Kane for an action-packed story about a heroine who must turn to a tough-hearted FBI operative when she's targeted by a stalker in *Bodyguard/Husband*.

A homecoming unveils a deadly conspiracy in *Unmarked Man* by Darlene Scalera—the latest offering in our new theme promotion BACHELORS AT LARGE. And finally this month, 'tis the season for some spine-tingling suspense in *The Christmas Target* by Charlotte Douglas when a sexy cowboy cop must ride to the rescue as a twisted Santa sets his sights on a beautiful businesswoman.

So gather your loved ones all around and warm up by the fire with some steamy romantic suspense!

Enjoy,

Denise O'Sullivan
Senior Editor
Harlequin Intrigue

BODYGUARD/ HUSBAND

MALLORY KANE

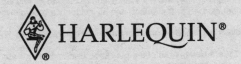

TORONTO • NEW YORK • LONDON
AMSTERDAM • PARIS • SYDNEY • HAMBURG
STOCKHOLM • ATHENS • TOKYO • MILAN • MADRID
PRAGUE • WARSAW • BUDAPEST • AUCKLAND

ISBN 0-373-22738-8

BODYGUARD/HUSBAND

Visit us at www.eHarlequin.com

Printed in U.S.A.

ABOUT THE AUTHOR

Mallory Kane took early retirement from her position as assistant chief of pharmacy at a large metropolitan medical center to pursue her other loves, writing and art. She has published and won awards for science fiction and fantasy as well as romance. Mallory credits her love of books to her mother, who taught her that books are a precious resource and should be treated with loving respect. Her grandfather and her father were both steeped in the Southern tradition of oral history, and could hold an audience spellbound with their storytelling skills. Mallory aspires to be as good a storyteller as her father. She loves romantic suspense with dangerous heroes and dauntless heroines. She is also fascinated by story ideas that explore the infinite capacity of the brain to adapt and develop higher skills.

Mallory lives in Mississippi with her husband and their dauntless cat. She would be delighted to hear from readers. You can write to her c/o Harlequin Books, 233 Broadway, Suite 1001, New York, NY 10279.

Books by Mallory Kane

HARLEQUIN INTRIGUE
620—THE LAWMAN WHO LOVED HER
698—HEIR TO SECRET MEMORIES
738—BODYGUARD/HUSBAND*

*Ultimate Agents

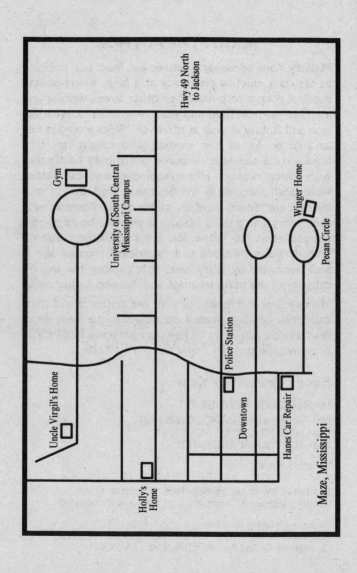

Hwy 49 North
to Jackson

Gym

University of South Central
Mississippi Campus

Winger Home

Pecan Circle

Uncle Virgil's Home

Police Station

Downtown

Hanes Car Repair

Holly's
Home

Maze, Mississippi

CAST OF CHARACTERS

Holly Frasier—Three men are dead because they cared for her. Now she's married to a stranger who swears he can protect her from her deadly admirer.

Jack O'Hara—This FBI special agent—known as the Ice Man—never lets his personal feelings get involved. He knows his strength is in his detachment. But Holly Frasier may melt his ice-encrusted heart, if he can keep her alive.

Virgil McCray—Chief of police of Maze, Mississippi. He only has the best interests of his grandniece Holly at heart.

Debi McCray—Holly's younger sister is afraid Holly will leave her alone to care for their great-aunt and great-uncle.

Stanley Hanks—The university gym's maintenance man has a special place in his heart for Holly.

Bob Winger—The town's high school English teacher depends on Holly to listen to all his problems, and solve them for him.

Donald Sheffield—Holly dated him for a short while, but he assumed they had a relationship, and he didn't want to let her go.

Earl Isley—An insurance agent in Maze, he wrote large insurance policies on both Holly's dead husband and her missing fiancé, with Holly as beneficiary.

Mitch Decker—Special agent in charge of the Division of Unsolved Mysteries, Decker treats all of his staff like family.

Eric Baldwyn—The division's profiler. He's got an uncanny talent for delving into the psyche of the killer.

Danny Barbour—Jack's best friend, and a detective in Maze who died from anaphylactic shock after a wasp sting.

For Joyce, who understands why.

Chapter One

Sunday, June 22

> "Love, if you knew the light
> That your soul casts in my sight,
> How I look to you
> For the pure and true
> And the beauteous and the right."

My heart was heavy as I watched you leave a fortnight ago. The days have been so long, the nights so empty since you've been gone. I live for your smile. I cherish your sweet, gentle ways.

You looked like an angel as you said goodbye, your hair as soft and shiny as a child's, and your white blouse glowing in the sun. You should always wear white.

But, Holly, you looked so sad. I know you hated to go. Don't worry, my dearest love. I'm here. I'll watch over you just like I always have. Every moment you've been gone has been like an eternity to me. This has been the longest two weeks of my life. But you will be back tomorrow,

and my world will be whole again. I know you've
kept your promise not to let one of those evil men
sway you ever again. Not one of them ever cared
for you like I have. You know I'm right. You
belong with me.

DON'T BE HIM, don't be him, don't be him, Holly Frasier
intoned as the man rushed into the airplane's cabin,
his tie flapping and sweat dotting his brow. Her heart
thrummed in rhythm with the idling engines. Paper
crackled as her fists clenched around the in-flight magazine she held but hadn't looked at.

Was this the FBI agent who was supposed to have
met her yesterday, then hadn't shown up? He looked
too young and disorganized, more like a fresh, eager
MBA graduate than a man who made his living sneak-
ing around and packing a gun.

Holly sat frozen, as if being perfectly still would
render her invisible, as he squinted at the seat numbers,
paused beside her row, then passed her by.

Taking her first breath since he'd stepped into the
cabin, she looked at her watch. Past time for takeoff.
Maybe the agent wouldn't show. With that thought her
neck muscles immediately relaxed. He'd already
missed their *wedding.*

After waiting all morning at City Hall in Chicago
as instructed, Holly had received a curt phone call
from the FBI field office. She was to board her late-
afternoon flight back to her hometown of Maze, Mississippi, from Chicago as planned.

That was it. No explanation. No information about
why the FBI agent hadn't shown up, or even if he
would.

Holly couldn't decide which was stronger inside her,

anger or relief. The two weeks she'd just spent in Chicago had been absolutely miserable. Although she'd done her best to enjoy the physical fitness symposium she'd attended, she hadn't been able to ignore the spectre of the meeting that loomed at the end of the two weeks—a meeting with an FBI special agent who thought someone had killed three men she'd cared about and who was going undercover as her husband to catch the killer.

Holly wished she'd never shown the notes to her great-uncle, the chief of police of Maze. Virgil Mc-Cray had taken one look at them and contacted the FBI. At their request, Uncle Virgil had compiled a file on Holly that detailed the death of her husband six years ago, the disappearance of her fiancé last year, and Detective Danny Barbour's recent tragic death from an allergic reaction. He'd also sent them photocopies of the three creepy, anonymous notes that had referenced the deaths.

The flight attendant began closing the overhead compartments. It was time for takeoff and the agent hadn't shown up.

Holly's hopes rose, then quickly fell as another last-minute straggler entered the cabin. This one had a prep cut, a custom-tailored suit and a scowl. She'd hoped her new ''husband'' would at least be nice. This guy looked like he ate toads for breakfast.

Don't be him, don't be him, she whispered silently, without much hope. He was the television stereotype of an FBI agent. Good suit, bad haircut, a suspicious bulge in his jacket.

The suspicious bulge beeped, and he pulled out a cell phone and spoke two curt words into it. Then he insisted to the young woman a few rows in front of Holly that she was in his seat.

Someone came in behind him. Holly had a vague impression of long legs in jeans, and a light-colored sport coat. She tilted her head, trying to get a clearer view. The businessman finally sat down, leaving Holly staring at the blue-jeaned guy. When she met his gaze, her heart lurched and her mouth went dry at the intense glacial gray of his eyes.

No way was he the FBI agent. He was too casual, too good-looking, too *unconventional*. Weren't all FBI agents stamped from the same stiff wing-tipped mold?

But his eyes were on her and the set of his jaw didn't go with his casual stance. Dread pooled in the pit of her stomach.

She squeezed the ruined pages of her magazine. Straightening her back she deliberately returned his scrutiny. He was tall and lean, with broad shoulders tapering to an admirable waistline. As a physical therapist, Holly had a good eye for fitness, and it was obvious the T-shirt under his jacket hid an excellent set of abs.

He finally broke eye contact, his gaze casually sliding from one face to the next down the rows.

With a chill, she realized what he was doing. He was checking out all the passengers. She was sure he'd be able to identify each and every one of them later.

He started down the aisle, shifting his carry-on bag from his right shoulder to his left, his mouth tightening in a brief grimace that he quickly covered. He moved with an offhand grace that fit his clothes better than it fit his knowing gaze.

She studied him warily as he approached. His face was lean and strong, his beard-shadowed cheeks hollow. Lines creased the corners of his mouth, but they didn't detract from his dark good looks.

He turned his gaze back to her as he came closer, and she forgot everything except the ability of those eyes to freeze her in place as completely as a mouse under an eagle's stare. She lowered her head, pretending to study her magazine, feeling his hot scrutiny like a sunlamp burning the top of her head.

Don't be him....

He stopped directly beside her.

Holly peered up at him through her lashes.

Leaning down, he braced his hand on the back of her seat. "Sweetheart?"

Adrenaline shot through her, leaving her breathless.

It *was* him! She'd hoped for pleasant. She'd gotten a predator.

Her throat wouldn't work. She couldn't have spoken if her life depended on it. Licking her lips, she tried to concentrate on drawing air into her lungs.

"You're not still mad at me, are you?"

His voice was low and masculine, and held a note of irony that immediately raised her hackles. His finely shaped mouth turned upward at one corner as his eyes slid over her with that eagle-like intensity.

She heard a soft chuckle from the passenger in the window seat beside her, and felt her face burn. It was all she could do to shake her head.

He held her gaze for a beat. Holly could have sworn his icy glare flickered, softened, before he hefted his bag, with a soft grunt, into the overhead bin.

As he stretched, Holly realized her eyes were on a level with the front of his jeans. The very front of his jeans. They were nice jeans, soft and faded with age, shaped by many washings to fit perfectly on his lean hips and mold his long, muscled thighs.

Cool it, Hol. She forced herself to pull air into her lungs, trying to maintain objectivity about the muscles hugged by that faded denim.

He leaned down again and put his mouth near her ear. ''Move over to the middle seat.''

His warm breath against her cheek sent shock waves through her.

''I don't—'' she started.

''Now.''

She moved. He collapsed into the aisle seat, manipulating his seat belt.

''Thank you,'' he said, then leaned back and closed his eyes. A sigh escaped his lips as he relaxed. His arm brushed hers. She leaned slightly away, but his broad shoulders overflowed the tightly packed seats.

Holly waited for him to tell her who he was, what he was doing and where he'd been all this time. Every second that passed in silence ratcheted up her tension another notch. She gripped the magazine with trembling fingers, giving brief consideration to rolling it up and whacking him to get his attention. Reluctantly, she put it back into the seat pocket.

Why wasn't he talking to her? Was this a typical FBI tactic, keep everybody off guard? It sounded like something the FBI would do.

She studied him impatiently. His straight black hair was tousled as if he'd been running. His unsettling eyes were closed, the long lashes shadowing his cheeks. There was a hint of pallor beneath his tan, and his face looked drawn and tired. Had he been ill?

A twinge of compassion pricked her, but she strictly

admonished herself. She was worrying about him and he hadn't even bothered to tell her his name.

Finally she nudged him with her elbow. "Well?"

He opened one eye to a slit and gave her a sidelong glance.

She frowned. "Aren't you going to introduce yourself?" she whispered.

"Keep your voice down."

"Keep—? Look, from your very odd greeting, I *assume* you're the FB—"

Before she could even blink, two warm, callused fingers covered her mouth. He leaned close and she felt his lips move against her cheek as he whispered.

"Don't ever say what you were about to say." He skimmed his finger over her lips and across her cheekbone as he gently kissed the corner of her mouth.

Holly's breath stuck in her throat.

He'd kissed her! *Oh my God, he'd kissed her.*

She brushed at her cheek. His mouth was quirked in a slight smile, but his gray eyes held a warning. He raised his brows and nodded toward the woman in the window seat.

Was he telling her they couldn't talk? This was *not* going to work. She couldn't sit here for hours beside this man who planned on insinuating himself into her life and not even talk to him. She had too many questions.

What had Uncle Virgil gotten her into?

Resisting an urge to throw up her hands in frustration, she decided her only choice was to play along. He'd asked if she was still mad at him. She could easily respond to that.

"Well, honey," she said sweetly, "I don't know

where you've been, but we need to talk. You're late. Very late.''

Beside her, the elderly lady closed her book and leaned closer.

That irritating smirk stayed on his sexy lips for a heartbeat, then he sighed. ''Yeah, we should talk.''

He touched the arm of a passing flight attendant as a voice over the intercom informed them the plane was backing away from the gate. The attendant leaned down, and he whispered in her ear for a moment.

Next thing Holly knew, the attendant was sending her a conspiratorial wink and pointing toward the back of the plane.

''Let's go.'' He got up.

She had no choice but to follow him.

The attendant led them to the rear of the plane where the two seats of the last row were empty.

He gestured for Holly to sit in the window seat.

''No.'' She wasn't going to let him bully her out of her aisle seat again. ''I'd rather have the aisle seat.''

''I'd rather you sat by the window.''

She took a deep breath, prepared to stand up for what she wanted, but one look into those icy eyes and she gave up and sat down.

''What did you tell the flight attendant?'' she asked as he settled into the aisle seat.

''That we hadn't seen each other in weeks and I wanted some privacy.'' He absently rubbed his right shoulder.

Holly groaned. ''And what's the real reason you moved us back here?''

''I like my back to the wall.''

Holly stared at him. ''How covert,'' she murmured. She leaned toward the window, but still the fabric of his coat brushed her shoulder, an uncomfortable reminder of how close she and this stranger were supposed to be, or at least act.

Holly doubled her hands into fists on her knees. She was ready for some answers. "Okay, I've been in Chicago for two weeks at a seminar that I couldn't even enjoy because I knew that as soon as it was over I had to meet up with the FB— with you. I am tired, I'm ready to be home. I've hardly slept since I got here. And you're acting like a…a *secret agent* or something."

"I am a secret agent or something, and I told you to keep your voice down."

"I don't want to keep my voice down. I want to scream, but I generally try to restrain myself in public places." She gritted her teeth. "Now, do you think you could do me the courtesy of introducing yourself?"

He rubbed his face in a weary gesture, then leaned toward her. She resisted the impulse to retreat as a faint pleasant scent of soap and the outdoors filled her nostrils and his breath tickled her ear.

"Jack O'Hara, special agent," he whispered. "Your fiancé."

The quiet, ominous words sent a thrill of fear through her as the plane taxied toward the runway, moving her toward the point of no return.

This stranger really was going home with her. She clenched her fists tighter and swallowed against the panicked constriction in her throat.

"Relax," Jack O'Hara commanded softly.

Desperate to hang on to whatever control she could, she lashed out at him. "Where have you been?" she whispered fiercely. "Correct me if I'm wrong, but weren't we supposed to meet yesterday? Weren't we scheduled to get married or at least pretend to, this morning?'' The irony of the time frame didn't escape her. *Meet yesterday, marry today.*

"I got tied up with a case. Just got in from D.C.''

The weariness she'd already glimpsed in his manner had crept into his voice. He sounded exhausted.

Stop making excuses for him. She sat back and folded her arms. "Oh well, that explains it,'' she drawled. "You were holed up with the bad guys and had your secretary call me? This sounds like the beginning of a great relationship.''

She felt a little better. Clean, righteous anger washed away her panic. She let the anger grow, let it reach out beyond the FBI agent to encompass her great-uncle.

Uncle Virgil had manipulated her into this scheme to ferret out a killer she was working very hard at believing didn't exist. And naturally, he'd found the only FBI agent in the entire world who looked like he came from Hollywood rather than Quantico and who wasn't a stickler for routine and order and, by the way, appropriate FBI dress.

"Sorry I was late, but until a few hours ago I was lying in a ditch using a cell phone to negotiate with a man holding two kids hostage.''

The plane shuddered over a seam in the tarmac at that moment. Holly's throat closed up again and her jaw dropped open. "Oh,'' she whispered. His matter-of-fact description of what must have been a tense, deadly ordeal brought the reality of her situation into sharp focus.

He was a real FBI agent. He dealt in life and death on a daily basis.

She thought about the picture his words painted. "Did everything turn out okay?"

He nodded shortly. "Yeah. This time."

His flat tone sent a shiver down her spine. Yesterday he'd been in a battle to save children, and today he was here for a reason she couldn't put words to. Deep inside, where she didn't want to go, a niggling little voice whispered, *What if it was all true?*

What if there really was someone in her hometown who had killed her husband and her fiancé and even one of her uncle's police detectives because of his obsession with her?

Jack O'Hara thought so. That's why he was here.

The sick feeling that had enveloped her four weeks ago when the latest note appeared rose like bile in her throat. Three unrelated events, years apart, with only one common link…her. It was too bizarre. But then, so was sitting next to an FBI agent whose assignment was to pretend to be her husband.

The monitor suspended just in front of them blinked to life, and an annoyingly cheerful flight attendant began the litany of safety features. Holly pretended indifference like everyone else, but she gripped the armrests until her knuckles turned white, and hung on every word.

"Remember that the nearest exit may be behind you," the voice droned.

Holly glanced quickly over her shoulder, comforted by the Exit sign so nearby, and relaxed slightly, stretching her cramped fingers.

Closing her eyes, she tried to concentrate on the new theory of muscle regeneration presented at the seminar, the ding in her windshield she needed to get fixed…anything but the fact that she was about to be hurtled through the air at the mercy of a metal box with engines bigger than her car while sitting beside a man she'd met only moments ago. A man who was going home with her to live in her house as her husband.

She glanced down at his hands that would soon take hers and slip a ring onto her finger. They were large and capable looking, with long well-shaped fingers. The nails were neatly trimmed. His coat sleeve had slid up a bit, and his wrist looked kind of bony, but strong. She glanced up at his face, scrutinizing the hollow cheeks and the shadows under his eyes. Because of the hostage situation, he must not have slept in over twenty-four hours. Was that why he looked so drained?

"Well? Do I pass muster?"

She started, realizing she was doing it again. They'd hardly met and she was already drawing him into her world as someone else to worry about, to feel responsible for.

He smiled wryly at her. The curve of his mouth and the remembered feel of his firm lips against her cheek made her tremble inside like a schoolgirl. But his unsettling eyes, shadowed as old glacier ice, chilled her.

She felt her face growing warm. "You don't look much like an FB—"

He touched her mouth lightly. "Remember what I said?"

Nervously, she moistened her lips with her tongue and accidentally tasted his fingers. The soapy clean flavor of his skin sent shivers up her spine. He tasted like a man.

He jerked his hand away.

She bit her lip, embarrassed. "Sorry," she said, then

realized her apology could be taken more than one way. "No more mention of…that."

She sat there for a minute, staring at her hands twisted together in her lap, and hating the feeling of helplessness that enveloped her like a shroud. "This is so foreign to me. I don't know how to act. What to say. How is this supposed to work, anyway?"

"Did you recognize anyone on the plane?"

She frowned at his seemingly unrelated question, but he just leveled that icy stare at her.

"No. No one."

"Are you sure?"

"Pretty sure." She glanced around at the passengers, acutely reminded of how his gaze had scrutinized every face as he'd walked toward her. So different from the way she had entered. She'd been tense and preoccupied. "I really didn't notice."

"You need to."

His voice was low and hard. It rumbled through her like faraway thunder, a promise of a future threat.

"You need to be aware of everything around you all the time. You need to observe, analyze, catalog the information in your brain. The killer could be your grocery clerk, your best friend, your pastor."

Denial leaped up to shield her from the horrifying possibility of his words. She took a shaky breath. "I can't believe you're really going undercover as my husband. I think my great-uncle Virgil overreacted to the notes. He'll be seventy-three his next birthday and he's under a lot of stress right now. He's always been too protective of my sister and me. Those notes could just be from some sick person who wants attention. This is all Danny's fault." Saying his name made her heart ache. *Poor Danny.*

Jack stiffened beside her. "Danny?"

"Detective Danny Barbour. When he moved to Maze back last September, his first case was my fiancé's disappearance. Danny had the notion there was some connection between Ralph's disappearance and my husband's death. But Brad died in an accident six years ago. And Ralph probably just changed his mind about marrying me and couldn't tell me to my face. Now poor Danny's gone." She shook her head as a lump of fear lodged in her chest.

"Why would your fiancé change his mind? Were you two having problems?"

"No. Not at all. I guess I was trying to think of a different reason for him to disappear, other than—"

Saying it all out loud made the idea that the deaths were related more real, and Holly did not want to face that possibility. "What if it's all just a tragic coincidence? You'd be wasting your time. You might not even need to be here."

"That decision's been made," he snapped. "Your case has been turned over to the Division."

"What division?"

"The FBI's Division of Unsolved Mysteries cooperates with local law enforcement on unsolved cases. Usually homicide."

Holly processed that information. "So what about your hostage situation? That wasn't a homicide, was it?"

He stared past her for an instant, his eyes focused inward. Then his gaze brushed her face briefly. "Yes. The father killed his wife several years ago and stole his kids from their grandparents. We caught up with him yesterday."

"Oh." He kept blindsiding her with horrific visions, made all the more sinister by his matter-of-fact recital.

She didn't like anything about this scheme her uncle and the FBI had dreamed up. Jack O'Hara was obviously a dangerous man, experienced in dealing with atrocities she could not even imagine, and now he was telling her she was stuck with him.

Feminine steel crept into her voice. "So you think you're going to take over my life because you've decided this is an 'unsolved mystery.'"

Just then the loudspeaker announced that the plane had been cleared for takeoff.

Holly tightened her seat belt with trembling hands. She hated the loss of control she always felt in an airplane, but she couldn't do anything about that. However, losing control of her life to this FBI agent was something she was not going to allow. She could take care of herself. She always had.

It infuriated her that Jack O'Hara was using scare tactics on her, with his talk of killers. Danny had hinted that her husband's death and her fiancé's disappearance might not be accidental. He'd thought the notes she'd received were from an obsessed admirer, but so far as she knew, he'd never found any proof.

"Sweetheart, you need to relax." Jack took her hand as the plane picked up speed on the runway.

The rough warmth of his touch surprised her, as did her reaction. As irritating as he was, as unsettling as his reason was for being here, his hand cradling hers made her feel safe and protected. It was a vaguely familiar feeling, a memory wafting across her mind like an almost recognized odor. Her tall, handsome father holding her hand as they walked into church each Sunday. Holly had always felt proud and happy, but most of all she had felt safe.

"What are you doing?" she whispered, staring at his long fingers wrapped around hers.

"You're afraid of flying."

"How do you know that?"

He squeezed her hand, rubbing his thumb over its back. "You'd be surprised what all I know."

What was that supposed to mean? How much had Uncle Virgil told him? Everything? She didn't like the idea that her great-uncle and this stranger had discussed intimate details of her life.

"If you're trying to make me feel better, you're not succeeding," she muttered.

"You like to be in control, and when you're a passenger in an airplane, you can't be. You've felt that way ever since your parents died in a small plane crash when you were a child." He glanced past her at the window. "That's why you like the aisle seat. You feel safer there, more in control. It's why you take on so much responsibility."

She sent him a suspicious glance. He had just echoed her own thoughts. Somewhere along the line, while she'd been seeking a way to feel safe and in control of her life, her great-uncle and great-aunt, her sister and the people of Maze had begun to depend on her, and she had accepted the responsibility, hoping for their protection and caring in return. But the hollow fear that had been planted inside her when her parents were killed had never gone away.

"Thanks so much for the ten-second recap of my life, and especially for mentioning crashing. So why did you insist on the aisle seat? Are you afraid of flying, too?"

The corner of his mouth quirked upward. "No. There are too many things you can control to spend time worrying about the things you can't. You're my assignment. I always take your vulnerable side."

Sometimes that feels like every side, she thought, trying to extricate her hand from his grasp, but he wouldn't let go.

"You're creeping me out," she said.

"It's my job to know all about you, to protect you."

"That's what's creeping me out."

JACK O'HARA SAW the poorly disguised fear in Holly Frasier's eyes as she licked her lips. He had to fight to keep his gaze from lingering on her mouth. He ran the pad of his thumb along the back of her hand. Then he realized what he was doing, and stopped.

He hated to admit it, even to himself, but for the first time in his career, his assignment had him disconcerted. From the instant he'd first laid eyes on her, he'd been off his pace. He'd like to attribute it to exhaustion and the lingering pain in his shoulder, but he knew he'd be lying.

He just hoped it hadn't shown.

He'd been at this a long time, and not much surprised him anymore. But Holly had. She wasn't at all what he'd expected. The picture her great-uncle had sent him didn't do her justice. It must have been taken several years ago, possibly right after her husband died. Maybe it was the only one her uncle had.

In the photo she appeared small, fragile, with a lost look on her face. A sad look. She was thin, and her brown hair was carelessly caught in a ponytail.

Her expression in the photo reminded him of his mother, of other stalking victims who lived their lives in terror of the next event in the nightmare that wouldn't end. It was his job to take that terror away, to give them back their lives. On a visceral level, he knew it was more than his job, it was his passion. But he kept the passion tightly leashed, because he also knew that emotion crippled judgment.

The woman sitting beside him was nothing like her picture. She wasn't thin or carelessly groomed. Her short-sleeved sweater revealed well-defined arms and shoulders and round, delectable-looking breasts. Her hair was thick and chestnut-brown, as were the delicately straight, no-nonsense eyebrows above her amber-shot brown eyes.

He hadn't recognized her until she'd looked up and he'd spotted a hint of the sadness that shone so strongly out of the photo. It had disappeared immediately, replaced by wary curiosity, then irritation. But for an instant her brandy-colored eyes had reflected the look of fear that haunted his dreams.

Her fingers tightened around his, wrenching his thoughts back to the task of distracting her during take-off.

"So, Holly, you surprise me. I thought you'd be less…"

She bristled. "Feminine?"

Oops. He'd spoken carelessly and obviously struck a nerve. What had he been about to say? Less self-assured? Less attractive? Less of a woman? He shrugged.

"I'm a physical therapist, not a Russian weightlifter." She glared at him.

He cocked a brow at her. "You are definitely not a Russian weightlifter," he agreed. Then, too aware of her nearness, he shifted and casually let go of her hand. "We're in the air."

Her eyes widened. "I didn't even notice." She paused. "Thanks for taking my mind off the plane."

"You looked like you needed a distraction."

She smiled, and Jack stared. She really was lovely. He was puzzled by his reaction to her. She wasn't his type at all. She was a little too tall, a little too physical for him. He'd never been one for serious relationships, but when he dated, he generally gravitated toward petite blondes. Women who looked like they needed protection.

Still, no matter how capable and strong Holly looked, she was also human, fragile, female, and being victimized by a stalker.

A flight attendant held out a bag of peanuts, and he reached without thinking. A painful twinge in his right shoulder made him groan. He took the peanuts with his left hand.

"Did you just groan?" Holly asked.

"No." *Damn it.* He was dead tired and he'd been lying in ditches, driving, and flying in planes for the past twenty-four hours. His shoulder was stiff and sore.

She touched his arm. "Yes, you did. What's wrong with your shoulder?"

Jack shrugged off her touch. He didn't need sympathy. Just sleep. Being even marginally handicapped by injury pissed him off. "Slight on-the-job injury."

"Oh."

Another wide-eyed "oh." He shifted his gaze away, uncomfortably sure that she'd picked up on what he hadn't said. The on-the-job injury was a bullet wound.

Why did he get the feeling it wasn't going to be easy to pretend to be married to her? He'd be happier if she weren't quite so attractive or so determined to take care of herself. That combination called up a primal urge in him—the urge to protect.

Who was he kidding? The urge to procreate. He clamped his jaw and swept those thoughts from his head. His lack of sleep was eating into his usual detachment.

This was a job, he told himself, a job like any other.

Even as he thought it, he knew it wasn't completely true. Sure, he was the Division's expert on stalkings and kidnappings, the logical choice to handle this case. But the reason he was here was because he owed Danny Barbour. When Danny called four months ago, Jack had been in the middle of another case, the case that had gotten him shot.

By the time he'd recovered enough to respond to Danny's call, it was too late—Danny was dead. He'd let his best friend down, and now he was here to make it up to him.

It hadn't been easy to convince his boss that he was ready to be back on the job. Special Agent in Charge Mitch Decker made it his business to worry about everyone under his command, whether they needed worrying about or not. And he had made it very clear what he thought of Jack's determination to take this case.

"I'm impressed that you requalified in firearms so soon," Decker had said. "But I won't have a vendetta. Detective Barbour was your friend. You won't be able to maintain the detachment you need to find this killer."

Jack had calmly reminded Decker that he hadn't given Jack the nickname the Ice Man for nothing. Jack was known for keeping his cool, no matter what the situation.

What he didn't tell Decker was that he'd made a promise to himself the day he'd watched his mother die at the hands of her ex-husband, his stepfather. Even though he'd been only thirteen, he'd known from that moment what he wanted to do. He'd devoted his life to stopping violence against women wherever and however he could.

He flexed his stiff shoulder, then pulled a tin of aspirin from his jacket pocket. He dumped three into his hand, tossed them into his mouth and swallowed them. Not easy without water.

"I can't believe you just did that," Holly said, digging into her voluminous purse. "Were those aspirin? They'll eat right through your stomach."

She handed him a half-empty bottle of water. "Drink all of it."

Jack took the water and drank gratefully, a little disconcerted by her attention and concern. He looked at her sidelong and found her watching to be sure he finished the water. He'd like to say it was annoying, but the truth was, he could get used to it. He'd never really had anybody to worry about him. Even his mother had been too busy working or going out to concern herself with a kid.

Dismissing thoughts of his mother, he settled back and considered what he knew about the case.

The Division's profiler, Eric Baldwyn, had provided Jack with a personality sketch of the UnSub, FBI shorthand for an unidentified subject. Eric was a strange guy, but he was the best profiler Jack had ever worked with. He had an uncanny knack for nailing a subject's quirks and oddities, and his profile had made the difference in more than one case.

Jack would keep in touch with Eric throughout the case, working with him to isolate the most likely suspects in this worst kind of stalking case. Most stalkers never turned deadly, but Jack knew from painful experience that some could.

Eric had told him the UnSub fit the classic serial-killer profile in many ways. He was almost certainly male, probably relatively young, late twenties or early thirties. If he wasn't young, then he was emotionally immature, an underachiever in a job that didn't make a lot of demands on him.

Eric also thought the killer's fascination with Holly may have begun years ago, perhaps even in childhood, and that his erotomanic obsession had developed over a long period of time.

Thanks to Eric, Jack already had many pieces of the puzzle. Most of it fit with Jack's own experience. What he didn't have was the most important piece. He didn't know what that piece was, but he knew *where* it was. The vital information that would lead to the killer was locked inside Holly's brain.

He looked at the lovely young woman sitting beside him. He probably knew almost as much about her as anyone in her hometown. Her uncle had seen to that. Virgil McCray had given Jack a terse but vivid image of Holly. One that made more sense now that he'd met her. He hadn't been able to reconcile McCray's description with the photo he'd sent.

"Holly takes care of everything around here," Virgil had said. "There's nothing she wouldn't do for her family or her friends. Everybody loves her. We depend on Holly."

She looked like someone who could be depended upon. She had a determined lift to her chin, a hint of compassion and caring in her eyes.

But Jack needed more than the view of her that her family and friends saw. He needed to get inside her head, understand her from the inside, see people the way she saw them, look at the town through her eyes.

He had worked a couple of cases of women who'd killed their husbands or lovers, so he knew he couldn't completely discount Holly as a suspect. His gut instinct told him she was no killer. He never went by his gut, though. In his line of work, logic and facts told the tale. He'd wait for the facts.

Jack almost felt sorry for her, because he'd seen something else in her wide-eyed gaze. A determined innocence. He hardened his heart. Sooner or later she had to face the truth. It would fall to him to strip away that innocence.

He didn't realize he was staring at her until she squirmed, then lifted her chin.

"Why are you looking at me like that?" she asked, her voice full of strain.

He frowned. He could already see that she was not going to sit back quietly and let him do his job. Maybe it was time she understood the depth of the danger she was in.

"Tell me, Holly Frasier." He braced himself and fixed her with the stare that had unnerved more than one suspect. "Who keeps killing the men who love you?"

Chapter Two

Jack got the reaction he'd wanted from his bald statement. Holly's face drained of color and she lifted a trembling hand to her mouth.

He took her hand and squeezed it gently. "You're not going to faint on me, are you?"

She shook her head.

He pulled a small notebook out of his pocket and patted his shirt pocket. "Got a pen?"

Her shocked gaze was still on him. He waited. After a couple of seconds she groped blindly beneath the seat and dug into her purse. She came up with a pen.

"No, keep it," he said, handing her the notebook, turned to a blank page. "I want you to make me a list of every man you've ever gone out with."

"Every man— You think someone I dated killed Brad and Ralph and—?" Holly's brain reeled. Her heart pounded painfully against her chest. Jack's calm, matter-of-fact attitude was more disturbing than her great-uncle's worry or Danny's tentative questions.

She gave a little laugh, trying to ease her tension. "It'll be a short list."

He didn't react. "That doesn't matter. The names

on it do. Most stalkers are former lovers or boy-friends.''

"St-stalkers?'' The word sheared her breath. Her body felt flash-frozen. Danny had talked about an obsessed admirer, but nobody had ever said the word *stalker*.

Jack nodded without speaking.

Her hand shaking, Holly took the notebook and tried to make her fingers work. "Everyone since my husband died?'' she asked.

"Every man ever.'' Jack watched Holly as she bent over the paper and wrote. She was quaking so badly that the paper fluttered, but she didn't falter.

When she finally handed him her list, it was short, as she'd said it would be, but he was impressed. It was extremely neat and methodical. He liked that. She'd listed the names in one column, and in the next column she'd indicated who each was, and when and for how long she'd dated him.

He studied the names. First on the list was her husband Brad, whom she'd dated through high school, then married. Jack knew Holly had been married for six years before Brad was killed. And she'd dated Ralph Peyton for eleven months before he disappeared. His name was second on her list.

Then she'd listed three names Jack hadn't seen before.

"Tell me about Gil Mason.''

Holly sat with her hands twisted in her lap. "I dated him for a short while, several months after Brad's death. He's the pastor of the Baptist church. Married now, with a beautiful little girl.''

"Earl Isley? The insurance salesman?''

"I only went out with him once.''

Jack saw her hands tighten. "Does he call? Do you see him?"

She shook her head. "Not really. Of course, we run into each other. Everyone does in a small town like Maze. And he's Uncle Virgil's insurance agent, and mine."

Jack made a note. It might be normal to "run into each other" in Maze, but he wasn't taking any chances. Every tidbit of information was important, until he could prove that it wasn't.

He reread what she'd written beside the third name and his neck prickled. Now *this* was important. Donald Sheffield had asked her out a number of times, until she'd finally refused to go out with him again. He'd moved to Jackson several months ago, but he still called her occasionally.

"How often does this Sheffield call?"

She shook her head. "Not that often. Maybe once every couple of months."

"Why did you quit dating him?"

"I'd only been out with him a few times, and he started making assumptions, like we were a couple. He was new in town and he seemed lonely. I never should have gone out with him in the first place."

Jack winced at the words he'd heard so many times before. Classic stalking personality, and classic victim response. He sat up straight, reining in his gut reaction of anger. "This type of behavior can be indicative of a particular type of stalker called an erotomaniac," he explained, tapping the paper. "Persistent. Keeps calling. Won't take no for an answer. He thinks you two have a relationship."

Beside him, Holly shivered. "But we don't."

"Now, who have you left off this list?"

She frowned at him. "Nobody. That's everyone I've dated. I told you it would be short."

As she spoke, the whir of the plane's engines changed and the flight attendant's voice came over the loudspeaker. They were about to land.

"You've left off at least one name, maybe more." Jack held up his hand as she stiffened. "Not on purpose. But this is important. You have to consider everyone. You may not have thought of your encounter as a date, but he did. You think about it, and when another name occurs to you, tell me immediately." He closed the notebook and slid it into his jacket pocket. He'd call Quantico as soon as they landed, and have background checks run on these names. He had a killer to catch.

BY THE TIME HOLLY pulled into her driveway twelve hours later, she was done in, mentally and physically. How had Jack crammed so much into one day?

He'd dragged her off the plane in Memphis and rushed her off to Chancery Court, where a marriage license and a judge awaited them.

"You're not suggesting that we really get married?" she had asked in horror, drawing odd looks from the other happy couples.

Jack had pulled her into his arms and whispered in her ear. "If anyone checks, I want everything in order, including the record of our marriage. Especially the record of our marriage. In a small town like yours, word would spread like wildfire if we were living in sin."

Shaken more than she wanted to admit by both his words and his warm embrace, Holly did as she was told—signing forms, repeating words, saying "I do"

at the appropriate time. At some point Jack slid a ring
on her finger, and gave her one to slip on his. Matching
rings. He was full of surprises.

Then they raced back to the Memphis airport, where
a small jet waited to fly them down to Jackson. By the
time they picked up her car from long-term parking,
Jack was stiff and quiet. His exhaustion was obvious
in his white, pinched lips and his sunken eyes. When
she'd suggested that he try to sleep while she made
the hour's drive to her house, he didn't object.

She pulled into her garage and reached for the
driver's side door. The new wedding band knocked
against the door with a metallic *click,* an undeniable
reminder that, at least for the moment, she was connected to this stranger by the most intimate of bonds.
She glanced over at him. He was awake, his gray eyes
soft and heavy-lidded.

"Honey, we're home," she said.

He straightened and flexed his shoulder, then
climbed from the car. "Pop the trunk and I'll get the
bags," he growled, his voice gruff with sleep.

"Thanks, *dear.*" Holly opened the door into her
kitchen and was greeted with the smell of old food and
the blare of music peppered with gunfire from the living room.

"Damn," she muttered.

Jack came in behind her. "Go back to the car," he
commanded, setting the bags down quietly. "I'll check
it out."

To her horror, he reached behind his back and pulled
out a big gun.

"Whoa! Hold on, cowboy." She grabbed his arm.
"It's my sister." She looked up at him. "Tell me

you're not going to be waving that thing around town. Not very subtle, *honey.*"

He scowled at her. "Never grab an armed man."

She held up her hands. "No problem, sir."

He holstered his weapon, but when she started toward the living room, he stopped her. "I'll go first. Where's the light switch?"

"It's just Debi," she insisted, gesturing to the left.

He reached around the doorframe and snapped on the lights.

"Sheez!" Popcorn flew everywhere as Debi jumped up, scrambling for the remote control. Her hand closed around it and the din of ominous music and gunfire stopped. "You scared me to death, Hol! What happened to you? You're late."

Debi's hair, which was the same dark brown as Holly's but enhanced by a deep red rinse, was messily twisted into a pile on top of her head. She wore a droopy T-shirt over leggings, and her face, bare of makeup, was shiny and pretty, if thin.

"And it's midnight and you're still up," Holly countered. "Don't classes start tomorrow?"

"Oh, baby, who's this?" Debi had spotted Jack. "Mmm, did you bring me a present, Hol?"

Don't say it, don't say it, don't say it, Holly thought, intoning the mantra that never seemed to work for her. She cringed as Jack slid his arm around her.

JACK FELT THE RIGID SET of Holly's shoulders. He squeezed gently. He'd pulled her close to demonstrate their relationship, but her brittle tension made him want to give her something—he wasn't sure what. Not reassurance. At this point he didn't have any for her.

"I'm Holly's husband," he said, watching the sister's reaction.

"Husband!" Debi repeated, her jaw dropping. She glanced from Holly to Jack and back. "Husband? You've got to be—"

As the concept sank in, her features changed from shock and interest to resentment. Her face shut down and anger flashed in the brown eyes that were so much like Holly's.

Jack raised a brow. Her reaction seemed a little over the top. Where had that anger come from? And why?

"Um, y-yes," Holly stammered. "Jack O'Hara, this is my sister, Debi McCray. Debi, Jack."

Debi stared at her sister for a beat, then turned to Jack. "So you go out of town for two weeks to a seminar and come back with a husband, and a hunky one at that." She held Jack's eye but spoke to Holly. "Don't you think that's kind of dangerous?"

Jack released Holly and leaned against the door frame with his arms folded. "Dangerous?" he drawled, giving Debi a bland half smile as he analyzed her body language and her tone of voice. "Come on. I'm nice, once you get to know me."

Debi laughed uneasily and rooted around under the couch, fishing out a pair of Birkenstocks and a nearly empty microwave popcorn bag. She tossed the bag onto the coffee table and slid her feet into the shoes. Grabbing a book from between the couch cushions, she headed toward the door.

"I don't mean dangerous for her," she tossed back at him.

He straightened.

"Debi…" Holly's voice held a note of warning, but her sister ignored her.

"I mean dangerous for you," she said to him, flashing a dazzling smile. "You should've checked things out before you jumped into marriage with both feet. My sister seems to have a bad effect on men." She opened the front door and paused dramatically.

"They die. Watch your back, Jack." She waved at Holly. "Glad to house-sit for you, Hol. Anytime."

As the front door slammed, Jack glanced at Holly, curious to see her reaction to her sister's hostility.

Her face was set, her lips pinched. She looked at the door, a worried frown on her face. When she realized Jack was watching her, she drew her mouth into a crooked grin and sighed.

"Little sisters, what are you going to do?"

"She doesn't know about your stalker?"

"No!" She gave him a warning look. "I don't want to frighten her."

"I take it she doesn't know about us either."

"Of course not. Uncle Virgil told me not to tell anyone."

Jack nodded, satisfied. She took instructions seriously and literally. That would make his job easier.

She picked up the popcorn bag and a glass with one hand and straightened the remote control and a couple of magazines with the other, then headed for the kitchen.

Jack followed and found her fumbling with the garbage bag ties, her hands shaking.

"Give me that," he said. He took the bag out to the garage. When he came back in, she was putting a stack of dirty dishes into the sink. She looked up, her amber-brown eyes glimmering with a touch of the sadness he'd seen in her photo. It tugged at a place inside him that he thought had turned to stone years ago.

Holly was different from many stalking victims he'd dealt with. For one thing, she was alive, he thought wryly.

Most stalking victims were all too aware of the danger that followed them everywhere. Holly's stalker had deliberately not revealed himself. Consequently she was trying very hard to pretend her life was normal. From the little he'd seen of her, she obviously spent a lot of energy hanging on to all the control she could grab.

As much to wipe the sadness from her face as to gather information, he asked bluntly, "What's going on with your sister?"

"Nothing you need to be concerned about." Holly turned away from Jack's icy, knowing gaze to run hot water into the sink. She didn't want to get into her relationship with her younger sister. Especially not tonight. She was too tired. He could whip out his suspicious microscope and study her friends and family tomorrow.

"I'm concerned about everything that concerns you."

Holly sighed. "You obviously don't have any brothers or sisters."

He didn't answer. She took that as a no.

"Debi was only four when our parents died, so she hardly remembers them. To her, I've always been the mother figure. She resents me telling her what to do. She's a kid."

"You'd been married for three years by her age."

"That's right." Holly nodded, unsettled by the extent of his knowledge. "And widowed within three more. But Debi's young, and I think she's afraid I'm going to go away."

Did the idea that Holly had impulsively married a stranger frighten her sister? Holly would have sworn she'd seen a flash of tears in the brown eyes so much like her own.

Jack studied her. "Pretty insightful. So what she said doesn't bother you?"

The tension of the past hours and days bubbled to the surface. "Sure it bothers me. But she's just lashing out because she's scared. I'm the big sister. It's my job to take care of her. And I do *not* want her involved with this." Now her own eyes were filling with tears. She blinked them away, along with memories of Debi's little hand squeezing hers as they cowered in the grim church sanctuary with the twin caskets of their parents looming over them. Eleven-year-old Holly had comforted her baby sister, but she'd wished desperately for someone strong enough to hold *her* hand and make *her* feel safe.

As if he'd heard her unspoken wish, Jack reached out, but stopped just short of touching her arm. "So, do you spend a lot of your time taking care of people?"

"What do you mean? Did Uncle Virgil tell you that?" She stepped away from the promise of his touch. She'd only known him a few hours. It disturbed her that she already knew the feel of his lips and the strength of his arms. Knew them and wanted to feel them again.

"It's obvious. Your fear that he's too stressed. Your relationship with your sister, your immediate concern about my shoulder."

Holly looked at the stranger who had been thrust into her life. He was too close, too big, too perceptive. He wasn't as muscular as Brad had been, nor as tall as Danny's six feet two inches, but he filled up her kitchen with his broad shoulders and his chameleon-like eyes, which seemed to be able to pierce through all her defenses, down to the heart of her.

She plunged a stack of dirty dishes into the soapy water, wishing she could wash away the past and all the heartache that had brought her to this point.

"You can put your stuff in the guest room," she said dismissively. "Second door down the hall on the left. The bathroom is the first door."

Jack didn't move. She felt his eyes boring into her back.

"Why did you get married right out of high school?" he asked, his voice gentle and low.

The question startled her. She rinsed a plate as she tried to think how to answer. She didn't want to talk about why she'd gotten married so young. "I thought you knew everything about me."

"I didn't say I knew everything. I said you'd be surprised what all I know."

Holly slung soap and water off her fingers. "So, since we're married, shouldn't I know all about you, too?"

He held her gaze for a beat. "This is about you, not me," he said. "I'm just the bait. You're the key. You didn't answer my question."

The bait. A thrill of apprehension ran through her. She got the feeling his questions were going to become a lot more personal and probing before he was done. "First of all, it wasn't right out of high school. We'd been in college a year. Besides, haven't you heard? All southern girls marry their high school sweetheart and have bunches of babies—" Her voice cracked.

"Were you happy?"

The three words struck her right in the middle of her chest.

"Happy?" She forced a small laugh. When had she thought of her own happiness? "Sure, I guess I was happy. I was in love. I was free." She gripped a soapy plate so hard she was surprised it didn't break.

"Free? That's an interesting take on marriage."

"I just meant I was on my own. Away from my aunt and uncle. Away from my sister. Away—" She stopped. Away from the endless weddings and funerals and baby showers that make up the social life of a small southern town, away from Aunt Bode's implying that she'd given up her freedom to take in Holly and Debi, away from the constant struggle to hold on to the little bit of control that made her feel safe.

"That sounds awful, doesn't it? Wanting to be away from my family? But I loved the idea of having someone to take care of me, instead of being the one everyone depended on."

"But then Brad died."

A place deep inside her began to hurt. She realized that as dynamic and handsome as Brad had been, all she remembered now was him lying pale and still in that mahogany coffin. She sent Special Agent Jack O'Hara a sidelong look. "That's right. He died and I was left alone. I had to come back home and—" And what? Become strong, dependable Holly again? The one who had all the answers, who took care of all the problems? Who never asked for help but always gave it?

"Who might have wanted Brad out of the way? How many hearts did you break when you married him?"

"Hearts?" She laughed shortly. "Me? None. Brad

was Maze's big football hero. Everybody loved him. Nobody hated Brad.''

"This isn't about hating Brad. It's about wanting you."

She shuddered. "Who would want me badly enough to—? It doesn't make any sense. How can Brad's accident six years ago be connected to Ralph's disappearance last year and Danny's allergic reaction?" She hugged herself, wishing she could encase herself in a cocoon of innocence, and not have to face the reality of her situation, the reason Jack was here.

"You're looking at the events through the veil of time and grief. I'm looking at them without prejudice, without feelings getting in the way." His words were dispassionate, but his tone was still gentle. She longed to wrap herself in that low, dark voice and never be afraid of anything again, but she knew that wasn't possible.

"You want me to believe they're dead because of me."

"Not because of you. You're as innocent as they were. You're the target of a stalker who must be stopped before he kills again."

Holly met Jack's cold gaze. Could he stop the killer? Or would he end up as the fourth victim?

He grabbed his bags. At the kitchen door, he paused. "You know, Holly, I'm not going to go away."

His words slashed all the way through to her innermost self, revealing the fear that was branded on her soul.

"Well, if you don't, you'll be the first."

"Then, I'll be the first." He headed down the hall.

Holly watched his retreating back. His shoulders looked no less broad from behind, and his hair curled where it lay over the collar of his jacket. She let her eyes drift downward to the slight bulge of the gun at his waist, and a chill slid up her spine.

The nightmare was real, as was the danger. There was a killer out there, and Jack O'Hara was here to catch him. Holly prayed that he could.

Holly picked up the last two plates Debi had left, and set them down in the water. At least some things never changed. She was still cleaning up after her baby sister.

The ring on her finger felt strange as she scrubbed the dishes. She looked at it. It gleamed and sparkled, lending its light to the bubbles that played around her fingers. The pad of her thumb rubbed across the smooth metal. She and this stranger were married in every legal sense. How long would they have to keep up this pretense? What would they say to each other, in public and in private?

She dried her hands, careful not to let the ring slip off. It was loose. She'd have to get it sized. She sank down in a chair and splayed her fingers on the clean white surface of the kitchen table.

Get it sized? What was she thinking? This was temporary. It wouldn't be on her finger long enough to matter.

She looked out the window at the quiet little street where she lived and felt exposed. Nausea burned the back of her throat as she considered that someone might have been watching her, following her for years. Even though Jack had assured her it wasn't her fault that the stalker had chosen her as his obsession, Holly felt a horrifying responsibility for everything that had happened.

A car drove by her window, and suddenly, Holly

wanted the blinds closed for the first time since she'd lived in the house. She jumped up and reached for the cord. The blinds were as old as the house, so the cord was frayed and tended to stick.

She tugged and wriggled it, but nothing happened.

"Here, let me." Jack's dark voice was close behind her.

She jumped. She hadn't heard him come in.

"They're old," she said inanely, as he reached around her to free the snagged cord.

Suddenly he froze. He was standing right behind her, his clothes brushing hers, his arm reaching over her shoulder, his breath lifting strands of her hair. It was an incredibly awkward and intimate position.

And he wasn't moving. Holly couldn't move either. The clean soapy smell of him wafted across her nostrils. The just-showered warmth of his body seeped through her clothes, through her skin. He was closer to her than any man had been for a long, long time, stirring yearnings inside her that she'd almost forgotten were there.

Finally he backed up and lowered his arm carefully, rubbing his shoulder.

She faced him. "Your shoulder's bothering you."

"It's tightening up," he muttered. "I haven't been able to work out the last couple of days to keep it loose."

"Why don't you let me massage it a little and show you a couple of stretches to help ease the discomfort?" She could deal with a stiff shoulder more easily than with the feel of his hard body against hers.

"I know the exercises. It's fine."

Holly found herself struggling not to smile. Was he actually anxious to get away from her? "Okay, Agent

Macho. But with those muscles all tied up in knots you won't sleep a wink.''

He shot her a venomous glare. ''That's Special Agent Macho. And I'll manage.''

Her smile widened as he retreated another few steps. So, he had a sense of humor. She took her first good look at him since he'd come back into the room. After his shower he'd pulled on a pair of exercise pants and a clean T-shirt, and he was barefoot.

Her smile faded. He looked stunningly sexy. His lanky frame was not as bulky as the jacket and jeans had made it appear. Her gaze slid down his body, past his tight, hard abs and muscled thighs to his feet. They were long, bony, masculine feet. Sexy feet. She swallowed.

''So, would you like coffee? Or some wine?'' she croaked.

Jack was relieved that she'd stopped trying to touch him. His jaw hurt from clenching as he fought to control his body's reaction to her. He'd already made a mental note to close the blinds, so he'd been only too happy to help her. A stalking victim shouldn't give the stalker anything to feed his obsession, not even a glimpse inside her house.

But he shouldn't have reached around her. First his damn shoulder had caught, then, before he knew it, her firm round backside was pressing against him, and his body was reacting, immediately and strongly.

In a sense it was gratifying. For the first time since he'd been shot, he'd reacted to a woman. But to be sexually attracted to Holly Frasier was inappropriate. She was his assignment, his responsibility. He had hard-and-fast rules about that. He never got emotionally attached to the victim or their family. Emotions impaired judgment, slowed reaction time, blurred goals.

He really needed some rest, and some distance from her.

''Jack? Coffee?''

He blinked, then nodded. ''Yeah. Coffee would be great.''

''Okay. As soon as I finish loading the dishwasher.''

She worked quickly and efficiently, rinsing dishes and placing them, just so, in the rack.

''Didn't you just wash those dishes?''

''Some of them had been sitting for days.''

''But you just scrubbed them, so why put them in the dishwasher?''

She sent him a sidelong glance. ''Because it's my house.''

He smiled to himself and leaned against the counter, watching her. He told himself he needed to know her, inside and out, in order to protect her.

As he'd noticed on the plane, she was in excellent physical condition. Her arms and shoulders were delicately muscled. Her tummy was flat and firm below gently rounded breasts. He already knew she had a great backside—he'd felt it, and the fitted black slacks she wore confirmed it. If the trend continued, her thighs and calves would be just as shapely and firm.

His body tightened again. He wiped a hand over his evening stubble and, with great effort, pulled his gaze away from her body.

Control, Ice Man.

His gaze was caught by a flashing red light on her telephone. ''You have phone messages.''

She looked up and sighed. ''I thought Debi was going to check them for me.''

''Check them now.''

She shot him a look that plainly said she didn't like him telling her what to do in her own house, but she pressed the button.

''Holly, it's Bob. I know you're not coming back until Sunday night, but could we meet for lunch on Thursday? I really need to talk to you.''

''Who's Bob?'' Jack asked, his interest piqued, but Holly just deleted the message and went on to the next.

It was a telemarketer. She deleted the message.

''Holly, it's Bob again. Maybe we could get together Wednesday instead. Have lunch at Benson's Restaurant. Please call me as soon as you get back.''

She pressed Delete. That was the last one.

''Who is Bob and what's that about lunch?''

''He teaches at the high school. We have lunch together every couple of weeks. Bob has a lot of issues and he says I'm a good listener.''

Jack rubbed his neck in frustration. ''Issues. What kind of issues?''

''You know, problems with his mother, problems with…dating. Stuff like that.''

''You didn't put him on your list.''

''I've never gone out with him.''

''Then, what do you call those lunches?''

''Lunches.'' She sent him a challenging glare.

''See, this is what I was talking about. You may think they're just lunches, but this guy sounds pretty desperate. Maybe he, like Sheffield, thinks you two have a relationship.''

Holly opened her mouth to protest, but Jack shook his head. ''Now, is there anyone else you've neglected to mention?''

She frowned and lifted her chin a fraction of an

inch. "No, or maybe I should say, not that I can recall right now."

Jack ignored her sarcasm. He knew it was difficult for victims to understand the depth of obsession that could lead to stalkings. She'd given him every name she could think of. He'd already known he'd have to dig for some of them.

"What's Bob's full name?"

"Robert Winger. Jack, he's very shy. What are you going to do?"

"Add his name to the list you gave me. I'm having a background check run on each of them." He'd call Decker first thing in the morning and add Winger's name.

His stomach growled, reminding him he hadn't eaten in hours. "I don't suppose you have anything to eat, do you?"

"Old popcorn," she said dryly as she filled the coffeepot. "I've been gone for two weeks and Debi never cooks. It's remotely possible there's bread for toast."

He flexed his shoulder and neck. He hadn't managed to cadge more than three hours of sleep in the past twenty-four. "Want me to see what I can find?"

"Sure, but don't get your hopes up. You'll probably take your life in your hands opening the refrigerator."

He stepped behind the counter into the small space of her kitchen. She'd taken off her shoes, and he noticed that she wasn't as tall as he'd thought. Her head came up to his chin, she was not that much taller than the women he usually dated. But there was a strength, an assurance in the way she carried herself that made her seem larger than she was.

He considered his thoughts as he opened her refrigerator and peered inside. The words his brain had conjured to describe her were not words he normally associated with women. Still, they fit her, and intrigued him.

Her refrigerator held the usual staples of a person who lived alone, plus the obvious signs of a messy houseguest. Besides the basic condiments and soft drinks and bottled water, there were stained Chinese takeout boxes, a half-eaten pizza and packets of soy sauce strewn over the shelves.

Grabbing a package of single-wrapped American cheese and a squeeze-bottle of margarine, he nudged the door closed with his hip. He'd have preferred an imported sharp cheddar and real butter. It was obvious he'd be doing the grocery shopping while he was here.

"Where's that bread?"

Holly was staring into a cabinet. She closed it and opened another one. "Hmm?"

"Bread."

"Oh. Left side of the freezer, toward the back. There should be half a loaf."

He found the package of sliced sourdough bread exactly where she had said it would be. Within a few minutes he had produced two plates of spiced, melted cheese over toast triangles.

"Here we go. Pour the coffee." He took the plates to the table and sat down.

Holly still seemed distracted when she sat. Then she looked at the plate for the first time. "What *is* this?"

"Welsh rarebit." Jack stuck a forkful into his mouth.

"Well, I'm impressed. Not only can you cook, you can make something out of nothing."

He shrugged. "I like to eat and I've lived alone for a long time."

She nodded absently as she pushed back from the table and went over to peer inside the dishwasher she'd just finished loading. Then she propped her fists on her hips and frowned as her gaze swept the kitchen.

Jack eyed her. "What's wrong?"

"You didn't hear broken glass rattling in that garbage bag you put out, did you?"

"Nope. Why? D'you lose something?"

Holly came back and sat down, her eyes troubled. "I can't find my favorite cup. It was the last piece I had of my mother's good china. I hope Debi didn't break it and hide the evidence."

Jack's pulse sped up. Her favorite cup was missing? Was it an accident? Or was the stalker collecting mementos?

Chapter Three

Jack ate his rarebit, pretending casual interest as he mentally went over everything he'd seen since he first entered Holly's house. There were no signs of a break-in. And as meticulous as she was, she would have noticed anything out of place.

Holly pushed her hair back, and Jack saw a faint glimmer of tears in her eyes. "Maybe I just misplaced it. I hope so. I loved that cup."

He tightened his grip on his mug, resisting the urge to touch the corner of her eye and catch the tear that clung there. What the hell was the matter with him? He'd never in his life thought about stopping a woman's tear with his finger. He'd never felt the slightest attraction to an assignment. He must really be tired. He concentrated on the missing cup. It could be a vital clue.

"Did everybody know how much that cup meant to you?"

"Everybody?" Her gaze turned sharp. "What are you saying? You think someone took it?"

He drank the last of his coffee, cursing silently. She was quick. He'd have to be careful. His question had reminded her that she wasn't safe in her own house.

He'd intended to use this first night to let her get used to having him around, become comfortable with him.

Too late now. This information was too important.

"Who has access to your house?"

She picked up her fork and drew circles in the congealing cheese. "Nobody, really. Debi, of course. And Uncle Virgil. I always lock my doors." She stopped.

He watched her, waiting. Carefully keeping his expression bland, he resisted the urge to prompt her.

She toyed with her food and took a sip of coffee. "You think this person who is obsessed with me broke in and stole my cup?"

"You don't seem like the type to lose things. You're methodical, precise. You leave nothing to chance. After two weeks away, you knew exactly where the bread was."

She laughed shortly as she picked up her plate and took it to the sink. "That's because Debi never looks in the freezer. She orders out. It's really not a big deal, Jack. I'm sure Debi broke the cup and threw the pieces away. Just forget it." Her eyes flashed.

"Have you misplaced anything else in the past year or so?"

She sighed in exasperation. "I lost a makeup kit a couple of years ago. I'm certain Debi borrowed it and never brought it back. I've misplaced Brad's class ring, but it's probably in a box somewhere. And I couldn't find a particular nightgown when I was packing for this trip."

Jack's skin prickled. "When was the last time you saw the nightgown?"

She wrinkled her brow. "Back in October. I bought it for—" Her cheeks turned pink and her eyes turned sad. "I'd never worn it."

"What color was it?"

She stared at him, confusion clouding her gaze. "W-white."

"And where did you keep it?"

Her throat moved as she swallowed. "In the second drawer of the chest in my room, on the right side under some…other lingerie. Maybe Debi…"

Jack watched her slow journey from disbelief to doubt. "Is that really what you think?"

Her eyes were on him, the doubt gone, replaced by fear. "You're telling me he comes into my house when I'm not here and takes things that belong to me."

He felt her silently begging him to reassure her, but he couldn't. He needed her to accept the reality of her situation, the reality of a killer who would do anything to possess her.

"Holly, there *is* someone out there who knows which of your possessions are most important to you, who watches you, who roams through your house while you're not here. The sooner you come to terms with that, the sooner we can catch the bastard."

He waited for her to crumple. Once stalking victims accepted the truth, they experienced an overwhelming helplessness and fear that sprang from a loss of control of their life. Some of them never recovered from that, even after the stalker was caught.

Her shoulders bowed and she gripped the edge of the counter as her face drained of color. Her eyes were huge, their golden-brown depths reflecting bewilderment and a flicker of panic. The corners of her mouth were white with tension.

He wanted to go to her, to gather her into his arms. It was an unfamiliar urge, an uncomfortable one. He'd received a few hugs from frightened or grateful victims, but he'd never in his life initiated a hug. He was pretty sure this was the first time he'd even thought about it.

"How does he get in without anyone seeing him?"

"He knows what he's doing. Your neighbors may even have seen him around and thought nothing of it. Remember, it's probably someone you know, someone your neighbors know."

Holly felt the words peppering her like hail, stinging as they hit. Her mug rattled as she set it down. She wrapped both hands around it, holding it still, using it to stop herself from shaking. "How—how likely is that?"

He shrugged. "It would be hard for a stranger to be inconspicuous in this town. Besides, this has been going on for six years, if we believe the notes."

"But Brad didn't die here. He died while we were living in Texas. It was an accident."

"And your fiancé disappeared, and Detective Barbour apparently had an allergic reaction. Seemingly unrelated events."

"Tied together by the notes." She didn't want to acknowledge that truth, but she couldn't help it. She shuddered. "I hate this! How can this person just come in and take over my life? Kill people I love? I can't stand it."

Jack reached across the table and put his hand over hers, squeezing gently. "Feeling exposed and helpless is natural."

"Not for me." She lifted her chin. She couldn't give in to those feelings. She was afraid if she did she'd fall apart like Humpty Dumpty. "I need to figure out who's doing this. I don't want anyone else to be hurt."

"The only thing you need to do is stick close to me and let me do my job."

She sniffed and shook her head. "I will not sit back like a southern belle on a verandah waving a paper fan while I wait for you to save me. I have to do something."

"You're doing exactly what you should be doing, pretending to be my wife. It's important that you act like nothing has changed. Don't forget, I'm the one he'll target, and we have to let him do that without arousing his suspicion. Because when he comes after me, I'll be ready."

Holly heard the steel in his voice and saw the cold resolve in his gray eyes. This was more than just a job to him. "Why do you do this?"

Jack's expression closed down and he dropped his gaze to his mug. "Do what?" he asked too casually.

"Set yourself up as a target to protect a perfect stranger."

He shrugged without looking at her. He obviously didn't like the question.

"It's my job."

"That's no answer. You chose your job. My question is why." This man who was so controlled, so professional, acted as if no one had ever asked him the question before, as if he didn't know how to answer. He shifted in his seat, then stood and took his dishes to the sink. He spoke without turning around, his voice remote and carefully even.

"Someone I knew was stalked and killed a long time ago. I decided I wanted to keep that from happening again."

"Oh, Jack…" She didn't know what to say. So this

wasn't just a job for him. He'd obviously cared deeply for whoever had been killed.

Before she could think of an appropriate response, he faced her, back in official mode.

"By tomorrow morning I need a list from you of everything that's gone missing in the past six years."

She stood and paced. "Why is this person doing this? You know all about stalkers. What does he want from me?"

Jack wished he could take her in his arms and calm her agitation and fear. But that would only help for a moment. He needed to stay focused so he could help her rid her life of this menace forever.

He crossed his arms over his chest, quelling the urge to reach for her, to comfort her. His next words would terrify her, but he hoped they would also prepare her for what was to come. "He wants to possess you. He may even want to *be* you. He probably has a shrine where he keeps pictures and mementos."

Her eyes filled with anguish.

"Pictures?" She shuddered and rubbed her arms. "How can I not know who he is? I know everybody in this town. They know me. These people grieved with me when my parents died. I treat them in physical therapy. I teach them in aerobics classes. I have lunch with them." She pushed herself to her feet and picked up her dishes.

Jack felt a jolt of compassion for Holly as the dishes she carried rattled against each other. He tried to make his tone comforting, because he knew his words were ominous. "That's the classic serial-killer profile. Most of them are quiet, unremarkable people. People you could live next door to and never know what they were doing."

He stepped aside as she went to put her dishes in the sink. Then, without thinking about what he was doing, he brushed a strand of hair away from her face. "We'll get him, I promise," he said gently.

Holly looked at Jack, at his straight, generous mouth, his sculpted cheekbones, his cold, determined eyes. She thought about the way he'd assessed and cataloged every single person on the airplane, his immediate suspicion about her missing cup. She believed him.

"Sure you will. I mean, that's what you guys do, right?"

His fingers lightly brushed her cheek. His eyes softened. "You better believe that's what we guys do."

The warmth of his hand went all the way through her. She had an urge to lay her cheek against his strong wrist, but she resisted. "Thank you," she said.

He raised a brow. "For what?"

"For being straight with me. For explaining things to me. I'd rather know what to expect than be kept in the dark."

He smiled, barely a movement of his lips, but she could see the ice melt in his eyes.

"There goes that need to be in control again."

She laughed softly and shrugged.

He reached to turn on the water in the sink and groaned quietly.

"Move over, gimp." She nudged him out of the way with her hip. The casual touch was like flint striking rock. It sent sparks dancing across her skin.

"I'll take care of the dishes," she said quickly. "It's after midnight and you need to put heat on that shoulder. There's a heating pad in the top drawer of the chest in the guest room. We have to be up early tomorrow.''

"Early? Why?"

Holly turned toward him, her hands on her hips. "Because the whole town is probably going to be on my doorstep at daybreak to check out my new husband."

Jack grimaced. "Small town," he said.

"Small *southern* town," she retorted. "Jack?"

He'd started toward the bedroom. He stopped and angled his head. "Yeah?"

"I don't know how to act with you. What are we supposed to do?"

His gray eyes sparkled as he grinned. Her heart fluttered. The transformation was amazing. His whole face lit up and his harsh features turned devastatingly handsome. She tried to focus on what he was saying.

"We're supposed to be married. So act like a newlywed. Remember, it's *me* he wants. His purpose is to keep you pure, by killing those who threaten your purity."

"You keep saying 'he,' as if you know."

Jack nodded. "Serial killers are virtually one-hundred-percent male."

"S-serial killers?" She started to shiver.

"Go to sleep. We'll go over to the police station tomorrow. I want to see the originals of those notes." He lifted his hand as if to touch her face, but instead he backed away and headed down the hall.

Holly stood there, his words echoing around her like a disembodied voice in a horror movie. *Stalkers. Serial killers.* How had her life gotten to this point?

"Oh, by the way."

She jumped. Jack stood in the doorway, his face planed in shadow.

"I put my stuff in the guest room, but I'll be sleeping with you."

Holly's throat closed up. Shock and panic raced each other through her body, all the way to the tips of her fingers and toes.

"You'll what?"

"We can't take the chance that your stalker might see anything that would tell him we aren't sleeping together. We're pretty sure he has access to your house. So everything must point to a happy newlywed couple. You have a king-size bed, don't you?"

Holly nodded slowly. She felt paralyzed. A vision of him in her bed, tangled in her sheets rose before her eyes. The inside of her mouth tasted like cotton and a thrill of something that felt a lot like fear streaked through her. She realized she was still nodding, and stopped.

Jack looked amused, which would have infuriated her if she'd had any room for more emotion.

"Don't worry," he said. "I'll stay on my side of the bed. I'm an honorable man."

JACK DIDN'T ENTER Holly's bedroom until he was sure she would be asleep. He'd walked through the house, turning off the lights, checking the doors, listening for any sound that might indicate that the stalker was watching. With the house completely dark, he peered through the living room blinds at the street, but saw nothing out of the ordinary.

When he eased open the door to Holly's room, the candles he'd lit earlier illuminated her bed like a pale spotlight. Her eyes were closed, her face relaxed in sleep. She looked young and untouched by the worries of the world. Her hair was spread across her pillow and one hand rested near her cheek.

Her innocence and beauty made his throat hurt. He stepped over to the window and peered through the blinds he'd closed earlier on his inspection of the house. He made a mental note to remind her to leave them closed.

He wondered as he blew out the candles what she'd thought about them. He'd lit them to lend a romantic glow to the room, so whoever might be watching from outside would see what was expected from a new husband and wife on their first night home.

He sat down on the bed and looked at the gold wedding band on his finger. It felt odd. He'd never worn a ring, and this one had bothered him all day. He twisted it, considering its symbolism. Although this marriage was only a cover, although he was Holly's husband in name only, he was sobered by the meaning of the vows he'd taken and what the ring represented. He'd vowed to honor and protect her, and he would do that with his life.

He lay down, acutely aware of the woman beside him, her soft breathing the only sound disturbing the silence.

He'd never had a long-term relationship with a woman. He'd never thought much about the rest of his life, but he'd always assumed he'd live it alone. Somehow tonight, that thought was not comforting.

He shifted, trying to relax his tense muscles. It had been a very long day, and from what he could tell, it was going to be a very long night. His shoulder ached, but that wasn't why he was wide awake. The image of Holly lying there, her face and arms golden in the candlelight, her hair spread over her pillow, was still burned into his retina like the afterimage of an explosion.

It was no leap to imagine being over her, his body molded to hers, bathed by her dark amber gaze as she opened herself to him. He threw an arm over his eyes in a futile attempt to stop the vision, and controlled his growing arousal by sheer force of will.

What the hell was wrong with him? He had never reacted sexually to a victim before. To him, stalking victims were to be protected, not lusted over.

Grimly, he recited the Code of Federal Regulations and ran his thumb along the smooth surface of the gold ring until he finally went to sleep.

Monday, June 23

> "So the chase takes up one's life, that's all.
> While, look but once from your farthest bound
>   At me so deep in the dust and dark,
>   No sooner the old hope goes to ground
> Than a new one, straight to the self-same mark."

Yes, love. Although at first a rage burned within me when I saw another defiler had turned your head, a new hope was born in me when you looked out your window into the darkness and saw me there, watching you. I watched as he forced you to close the blinds. You cannot come to me yet, I know. But it is still me you really want. Until then, my dearest love… "So must I see, from where I sit and watch."

HOLLY RAN ALONG the early morning streets, lifting her face to the breeze that evaporated the sweat from her skin as she stretched her gait and found her rhythm. It wouldn't be long before the south Mississippi air became as hot and suffocating as a sauna, but this morning it was invigorating. Green overhanging branches along the boulevards shaped sunbeams into pixies that danced on the ground around her feet as she ran. The air smelled faintly of honeysuckle and gardenias. The streets were quiet as the little town of Maze began to wake up.

But inside Holly, a huge argument was raging. When she'd woken up this morning, she'd been shocked to find Jack in bed beside her—until her sleepy haze evaporated and she remembered.

He was sound asleep, his thick eyelashes resting against his tanned cheeks, his hair mussed as if he'd been restless in the night, his breathing soft and even.

She'd watched him for a few minutes, fascinated by the beauty of his face and body. He couldn't be considered traditionally handsome, his features were too strong. But the curves and planes of him were harshly elegant, like the stark beauty of an untamed desert.

She'd almost touched him. The urge to trace his features, to slide her fingers along the sinewy muscles of his arm was almost irresistible.

How was she going to sleep in the same bed with him? His presence reminded her of how safe she'd felt with Brad beside her. And how lonely a bed could be.

She almost stumbled over a crack in the sidewalk. Taking a deep breath she admonished herself. *Pay attention. Concentrate on the rhythm of the exercise.* There was no future in dreaming about waking up with Jack at her side. When all this was over, he'd be gone.

Deliberately, Holly concentrated on her pacing, and

on the familiar houses and streets she passed. But it was all different today. A curtain fluttering in a window; Mr. Parr glancing up as he swept the sidewalk in front of his barbershop, a shout echoing through the early morning air. All sorts of things she'd never paid attention to before today seemed ominous, because she knew a stalker watched her. The thought that there was a killer living among her circle of friends and neighbors brought terror to her heart.

As she turned down Spring Street, she heard a car behind her. That wasn't unusual. Several of her neighbors went to work early. She always waved at them as she ran. She kept jogging, waiting for the car to pass and the driver to wave, but it stayed behind her, its engine whirring and the smell of exhaust tickling her nostrils as it slowed to keep pace.

She glanced around quickly, but all she could see was a dark blur. With the hairs on her neck prickling and her pulse hammering, Holly lengthened her stride, preparing to sprint the rest of the way to her house.

Suddenly, tires scraped against the curb and a horn blared.

Holly jumped and almost lost her footing. She felt the heat from the car engine against her leg.

"Hi, Holly," the driver said, rolling his car window down.

"Stanley!" Holly breathed deeply to stop the runaway pounding of her heart. It was just Stanley. He worked for the University of South Central Mississippi, on the Buildings and Grounds staff.

She propped her hands on her hips and waited for her breathing to return to normal. It irritated her that she was so jumpy. "You scared me. What are you doing on this side of town so early?"

Stanley's blue eyes skimmed her face, his plain, even features lighting up as he grinned at her. Holly relaxed. Stanley had always looked after her, walking her to her car at night after her aerobics classes, making sure there were fresh towels, helping her put away equipment.

"I'm so glad you're back. The ladies in your aerobics class are complaining about Coach Jones." He pushed a big-knuckled hand through his brown hair.

Sharing his laughter at the thought of Betty Jones, the women's basketball coach, leading her elderly aerobics class, Holly brushed damp strands of hair off her forehead. "Betty is disciplined, to say the least. I'll be there tomorrow night."

He nodded. "Good. Your ladies will be happy. Everybody missed you while you were gone. I heard a rumor, Holly, that you—" He stopped as his gaze slipped past her.

Holly followed his gaze. Jack was coming toward her, a coffee mug in his hand. Her heart fluttered at the sight of him. He sported a smile, but she could see it was forced.

"Good morning, sweetheart," he said with false cheerfulness as he came up beside her and kissed her quickly. "Who's this?"

Holly made herself link her arm with Jack's. "Stanley, this is Jack O'Hara, my husband. Jack, Stanley Hanks. He takes care of the gym at the university."

Stanley nodded, his grin noticeably absent. "Hi, Jack. Nice to meet you. Well, I'd better go. It's good you're back, Holly." His car pulled away from the curb.

"How the hell did you sneak out of bed without me hearing you?" Jack demanded as Stanley drove away.

She stared at him. He was dressed in crisp khaki pants and a white shirt. His hair was damp and combed, and his face was as dark as a thundercloud. How could he look so handsome and so angry at the same time?

"Good morning to you, too," Holly said to the back of his head as he turned to watch the disappearing car. *"Dear,"* she added pointedly.

"We agreed that you would stick close to me."

"No. You *decreed* that I would stick close to you. We didn't agree on anything." Holly blotted sweat from her brow, thinking about the irony of their conversation. "And I didn't sneak out of bed. You were obviously exhausted, because you were so sound asleep, a train wouldn't have woken you."

"The fact remains that you shouldn't be out here alone," he muttered.

"You'd better be careful in public, *honey.* Mrs. Ross will have it all over town by noon that we had our first argument right in front of her house this morning." She smiled and waved in the direction of Mrs. Ross's front porch, where that gray-haired lady stood ogling them.

"This isn't a joke."

Holly took a deep breath. "I know it isn't a joke. But if you want to be inconspicuous, you're not doing a very good job of it."

"I'd rather not attract attention, but that's not my first priority. Your safety is. Listen to me. You cannot go out alone. The killer could be anyone. You could've run past him this morning without even realizing it." He gestured in the direction Stanley's car had gone, still scowling. "It could be that Stanley guy."

She stared at him. "Stanley?" She looked down the

street, then back at Jack. "Stanley is sweet. He adores the little old ladies in my elderly aerobics class."

Jack looked at her sidelong. "From the way he was looking at you, I don't think it's the little old ladies he adores. Why wasn't he on your list?"

"List? Stanley? I've never dated Stanley."

Jack's sharp icy gaze studied her. A memory flashed through her brain, and she felt her face turn pink.

"Okay, he took me to the prom in high school, but that was only because Brad had injured his ankle. Brad told Stanley to take me so I wouldn't miss the dance."

"So you knew him in high school, and you *have* dated him."

"It wasn't a date." She crossed her arms and glared at him, noticing out of the corner of her eye that Mrs. Ross had stepped off her porch onto the sidewalk, probably trying to hear better.

"When I said I needed the name of every man, I meant *every* man," he said tightly, the pending storm back in his expression as he rolled his mug between his palms. "You don't decide whether to give me the name. You give it to me and I'll decide."

She blew her breath out in an exasperated sigh. "Does that include Sunday school teachers? Baggers at the grocery store? People I smile at on the street? Don't you understand? This is a close-knit community. I know everybody."

Jack scowled. "Be reasonable, Holly. But don't be careless. It could be anybody."

She squeezed her eyes shut. "Okay."

"And you don't go anywhere without me. Is that perfectly clear?"

"Yes, sir. But speaking of clear, the clear message your body language and the look on your face are sending is that you're about to chew me up and spit me out," she said, forcing a smile to her lips. "People are watching."

With an obvious effort, Jack relaxed his features and leaned over and kissed her brow.

She closed her eyes, wishing he would stop doing that. The feel of his firm-yet-gentle kiss was becoming altogether too familiar, too comforting.

"Is this better?" he whispered against her ear, sending shivers down her spine.

"Not really," she muttered as he pulled away.

"Holly. What I do is unusual. When I investigate an unsolved crime, the evidence is already cold. I don't have leads. I don't have clues. I don't have fresh victims or uncontaminated evidence. I can't work forward, so I have to work backward. In my world, everyone is a suspect until proven innocent. It's how I have to work."

She felt Mrs. Ross's interested gaze still on them. "If everyone in town is a suspect, does that include me?"

Jack didn't take his eyes off her. "You seem to have airtight alibis for the time of each death."

"Well, that's a relief," she drawled, noticing he hadn't really answered her question.

"Look. If I'm going to be able to protect you, you have to trust me. I know what I'm doing. But you have to do what I say and you have to stick with me."

The sunlight picked up highlights in his black hair and played off the planes of his face, somehow making him look less official, more approachable.

She believed he could protect her. His determined jawline, the glacial gray of his eyes, the strength of his fingers wrapped around the mug—all reassured her. He had a quiet control that she had fought all her life to attain. The fragile thread of determination that had kept her going since her parents' deaths was unraveling. If she lost that and had nothing to replace it, she was afraid she'd fall apart.

Perversely, she wondered if there was anything or anyone that could melt Jack's icy control. Eyeing him narrowly, she baited him. "You always get your man. Do you always rescue the damsel, too?"

His head jerked slightly as if he'd heard a shot or dodged a blow. Recovering instantly, he raised one brow and looked down at her feet, then let his gaze travel up her legs, past her running shorts and her sports bra, all the way up to meet her gaze. She saw a look in his eyes that disturbed and excited her.

A look of hunger.

She folded her arms over her Lycra-clad breasts, suddenly feeling exposed. Her nipples tightened and she licked dry lips, forgetting her question, until it occurred to her that that was precisely his intent.

She shook off the haze of desire and straightened, reminding herself of where they were. Mrs. Ross probably couldn't wait to call all her friends to tell them that Holly's new husband was undressing her with his eyes in the middle of the street.

"This is not a game, Holly. I don't want anything to happen to you."

He looped his arm around her, his hand resting on the curve of her hip. "Let's go inside. We've got an appointment with your uncle in forty-five minutes."

Knowing that every move they made was destined to be the subject of coffee-break conversations all over town, she gently but firmly slid his hand up to her waist.

She felt a rumble in his chest that could have been a soft chuckle.

"Watch how you act in public, Jack. This is a conservative town, and, like I told you, people are watching."

Jack leaned over and put his lips near her ear. "If we're lucky, that includes the killer."

Chapter Four

"The killer is stocking his love nest." Jack stood in the garage, talking to Decker on his cell phone.

"That's what it sounds like. Have you talked to Eric?"

"Nope. I left a message on his voice mail. Here's the rest of the list." Jack read off the disturbing items that Holly had listed as missing: a ragged stuffed dog from her childhood, Brad's class ring, which she'd worn on a chain around her neck all through high school, a ruffled pillow from her bed, a makeup kit. And that was just about half of the list. Combine these with her favorite cup and the nightgown that he was sure from her reaction was a fancy, revealing one, and anyone would draw the same conclusion. A deep, nauseated shudder rippled through him. He had to catch this bastard before he laid one hand on Holly. "When can Baldwyn get to these?"

"He's on a missing-child case right now, and you know how he is when he's working. But he ordered in some food earlier. That means he may come up for air soon."

"Tell him I want to know which of Holly's possessions the UnSub's going after next. And when."

"How soon do you need this? Like, yesterday?"

Jack laughed without humor. "Sooner. Now, what do you have on my suspects?"

"Let's see. There was nothing on the Baptist preacher, but Peyton, your vic's fiancé, took out a substantial insurance policy on himself shortly before he disappeared. Holly is the beneficiary. Of course, it hasn't paid out yet because Peyton is still listed as missing. The insurance salesman who sold it to him was Earl Isley. He wrote her husband's life insurance, too."

"Well, Holly didn't kill them for the insurance. So, you think Isley?"

"Maybe he plans on marrying into that money. It's been done before. The two policies together are seven figures."

Jack filed away that information. "What about Sheffield?"

"Now, *he's* interesting. Donald Sheffield is currently under a restraining order in Jackson. Seems he was a little too persistent with a young woman who tried to break up with him. Wouldn't leave her alone. Got physical."

Jack's pulse hammered in his temple. This could be his first real lead. "A restraining order. That's the guy Holly said tried to turn a couple of dates into a commitment."

"You want the locals to pick him up for questioning?"

"Yes. And I want to be there. Have them notify me when he's coming in. And thanks for the quick work."

"Thank Nat," Decker said. "She worked all night."

Jack smiled. Natasha Rudolph was, like all the

members of their elite team, the best at what she did. And considering what Nat did with computers, Jack never ever wanted to find himself on her bad side. He had no doubt that with a few keystrokes, she could wipe out all traces of his existence.

"Tell her thanks, and give her two more to check out—Robert Winger and Stanley Hanks."

"I'll tell Nat to get right on it. Now, I've arranged with the local field office to check in with you daily via your cell phone. And you've got their number if you need assistance. And remember, I can be there within a few hours."

"I know."

Decker's voice took on a new timbre, the tone of friendship. "Take care of yourself, Ice Man. I'll see you in a day or two."

Jack nodded his appreciation, even though his boss couldn't see him. "Make sure the locals understand how important it is that they call me about Sheffield. He sounds like a classic stalking personality. He could be our guy."

UNCLE VIRGIL LAID OUT the three notes like velvet jewel cases in front of Jack. Holly sat to one side of her uncle's ancient desk and refused to look at the plastic-bagged pieces of paper. She'd spent enough time staring at them. Their words were carved like surgical scars on her heart. Their presence made the unthinkable a reality.

Jack picked up one of the notes and studied it. He looked at the front, the back, held it up to the light and peered through it. He turned it upside down and stared at it, then righted it and stared some more.

Holly was fascinated. He was totally focused on the

piece of paper, his dark brows furrowed, his eyes narrowed. He carried it to the window, holding the plastic bag against the glass, as if the light shining through the paper could reveal a secret message or code.

His long fingers splayed against the window pane promised strength and gentleness at the same time. She'd known the man less than twenty-four hours and the touch of those fingers was already familiar to her.

She shifted uncomfortably. The day had grown warm. Uncle Virgil's air conditioner was older than she was, and since it was only June, her parsimonious great-uncle wouldn't even contemplate turning it on for another month.

Jack, of course, looked cool as the proverbial cucumber. The only wrinkles in his crisp white shirt were where he'd rolled up the sleeves, baring sinewy forearms with a light dusting of dark hair.

Forcing herself to stop ogling him like a teenager, she concentrated on what he was doing. He held up the first note, the one that had come after Brad died.

"'Dear Holly,'" he read aloud. "'Mere words cannot express my sorrow for your loss. Believe ye will not see him any more about the world with his divine regard! For all was as I say, and now the man lies as he lay once, breast to breast with God.'"

Taking a small notebook from his shirt pocket, he jotted notes. "How soon did you receive this after your husband's death?"

"I'm not sure. Within a few days. It was in with a stack of sympathy cards."

"Was it in an envelope?"

"I don't think so." Holly thought about those awful days after Brad died. "I wasn't paying much attention."

"And you don't recognize the handwriting?"

She shook her head. "It's so plain."

"Block printing. Most of the time it's hard to analyze." Jack took the note back over to the table. "Tell me how he died."

"O'Hara—" Uncle Virgil leaned forward "—you got all that info. Holly don't need to be put through this again."

"Sir, as a law enforcement officer yourself, I'm sure you can appreciate the importance of a firsthand account from someone close to the victim. I thought we understood that I was to be given complete cooperation."

The two men faced off for a moment, and Holly could feel the battle of wills. Two strong, stubborn men, each with his own way of doing things. Each in his own way protecting her. The sight gave her a warm feeling, a safe feeling—a feeling she hadn't felt many times in her life.

"It's okay, Uncle Virgil—" Holly began as the door opened.

"Chief." It was Theodore "T-Bone" Polk, one of her uncle's detectives. "Oh, hi, Miss Holly," he said, his weathered face turning red. "S'cuse me, but Miss Emma Thompson run into a telephone pole again. This time over at Cherry and Main."

T-Bone's gaze lit on Jack. "This the new husband?" He frowned and spared Jack a half-inch nod. "You better be good to our little Miss Holly or you'll have to answer to me."

Jack nodded easily, but Holly felt him stiffen.

"I'm s'posed to be in court in Jackson in an hour. I'm already late."

Virgil sighed. "All right, T-Bone. You get going.

I'll take care of Miss Emma. I reckon I'm either going to have to escort her personally to the eye doctor or take that precious fifty-nine Chevy of hers away.'' He looked at Jack. ''This is the third telephone pole she's hit this year.''

''Thanks, Chief. Miss Holly.'' The burly detective touched an invisible hat brim. ''Oh, by the way, Jeannie said she's ready anytime to learn those new exercises.''

''Okay, T-Bone,'' Holly said. ''I'll call her this week.''

T-Bone sent Jack a dismissive nod and left.

Uncle Virgil searched Holly's face. ''Holly?''

''I'll be fine. You go ahead.'' She kissed her uncle's weathered cheek.

He nodded tentatively. ''You'll come over tonight?''

She put on a smile for him. ''Of course. I'll fix dinner, and we'll let Aunt Bode meet Jack.''

After Virgil left, Holly looked at Jack. ''He's worried about me.''

''I know.'' Jack gave a brisk nod. ''Tell me about that detective who has a thing for you.''

Holly gawked at him. ''What? Are you talking about T-Bone?''

''He turned bright red when he saw you. Then there was his threat.''

''T-Bone? Threat?'' She thought back over what T-Bone had said and laughed. ''You mean about answering to him? That's just an expression. You're in the south, Jack. People take family and friends seriously. And they talk like that. Surely even you know that was no threat.''

Jack didn't crack a smile. "Has he ever asked you out? Made overtures to you?"

"T-Bone? He's married with two kids."

"That doesn't answer my question."

Holly sighed in exasperation. "No, *dear,* he's never asked me out. He's older than me. He'd graduated by the time I started high school."

"So had I."

She stared at him. Suddenly, Jack O'Hara moved a little bit closer to her universe. He wasn't just an FBI agent. He had a life, a past. He was thirty-two or thirty-three years old—four years older than her.

But there all resemblance between him and anyone she'd ever known ended. He was defined by his job, focused, serious, yet detached. He asked questions and filed away the answers like a computer.

"You cannot possibly think T-Bone is a suspect because he blushed. He's always gotten embarrassed easily."

Jack looked at her steadily.

"Oh God." She collapsed back in her chair. "You're going to do this to everyone I know. This is going to tear the town apart."

Jack shifted in his chair. "Holly, I know it's hard second-guessing everyone around you—"

"It's easy for you to say you know, but you don't. When this is all over, you'll just dust off your hands and go home. I have to stay here and live with all these people you're accusing."

"When this is all over, everyone will understand. They'll support you because you're one of them."

"You really don't get it, do you." She lifted her hair off her hot neck. "If what you say is true, then the killer is one of them, too. And no matter how it turns out, my life will never be the same. The last thing I want is people finding out about this. Offering casseroles and sympathy, walking around on eggshells as if they think I'm going to fall apart—or worse, let them down. Like it would be a big catastrophe if I was too distraught to organize the Wellness Picnic this year.'' She stopped, ashamed of her bitter outburst.

"Maybe it's how they let you know how important you are to them."

His words were awkward, but somehow more comforting than all the fussing and food her neighbors considered appropriate for sympathy.

Was she too hard on her friends and neighbors? On herself? Was she the only one who demanded the perfection and supreme organization she'd surrounded herself with?

"So, how did your husband die exactly?"

"Back to the business at hand," she muttered.

He looked up, but she shook her head. "Never mind." How had Brad died? Carelessly. Too young. "He slipped in the locker room shower."

"He was alone."

She nodded. "He'd been refinishing the gym floor."

"The autopsy indicated a broken neck and a massive contusion on the back of his head."

A twinge of pain began behind her right eye. She rubbed her temple, recognizing the signs of a migraine headache. "I know what the autopsy indicated," she said tiredly.

"But there was no investigation?"

She glared at him. "You know there was no investigation."

"Are you aware that the Medical Examiner noted that the appearance of the contusion possibly indicated a second blow? Or that there were questionable bruises on his neck?''

Holly's face drained of color. "Questionable bruises?''

Jack nodded. "Apparently your husband's family doctor said Brad was a hands-on football coach and could have gotten the bruises during practice.''

Holly looked down at her hands. Jack was turning her world inside out, speaking his devastating words in his calm, reasonable voice. "Nobody told me.''

Jack looked at her steadily. "Your uncle Virgil asked that you not be upset unnecessarily.''

"So there's no question Brad was murdered?''

"Our medical experts are studying the autopsy report.'' Jack pulled the second note toward him.

"'Dearest,''' he read softly, as if to himself. "'You deserve more than I can ever give. Oh which were best, to roam or rest? The land's lap or the water's breast. Do not grieve. I am always nearby. Remember, my dearest love, the best is yet to be.'''

Holly felt a chill run up her spine as Jack read the words.

"'The best is yet to be,''' he repeated, then wrote something on his notepad.

"Do you recognize it?'' Holly asked.

"Browning.''

"Of course.'' Her pulse sped up. "I thought it sounded familiar.''

His hair slid over his forehead as he nodded. He pushed his fingers through it absently. "'Grow old along with me, the best is yet to be.' Is there any significance to you, either in the words or in the fact that it's Browning?''

"No." She shook her head and got up. "I'm going to turn on this air conditioner, if it will even work."

She pressed the power button on the ancient window unit and sat back down as it lumbered to life, coughing out a mildewy smell. Holly raised her face to the cool, musty air. "I barely remember Browning from high school English. I thought he was kind of depressing and sappy."

Jack held up the second note. "How did you find this one?"

Holly sighed and closed her eyes for an instant. "I didn't. Danny did. He was investigating Ralph's disappearance and he found the note in with the wedding gifts I was returning. That was back in November."

"And Ralph had been missing how long?"

"Since early October."

"Less than two months before the wedding."

His flat tone spoke volumes, as usual.

"You think Ralph is dead, don't you. Do you think he was killed so…so I wouldn't marry him?" Holly had admitted that possibility to herself, but she'd never said it out loud.

Jack nodded, hating to quash her thread of hope. "We're pretty sure he's dead."

"But what about Danny? What was the point in killing him?"

That was the question that had plagued him. "You didn't put Danny's name on your list either. Were you and he seeing each other?"

"No! I mean, we were friends. He was investigating Ralph's disappearance and he helped me a lot." Holly paused.

Jack saw her eyes shining with unshed tears. Had she been in love with Danny? A vision of Holly and

Danny together flashed through his brain. He clamped his jaw.

God knew anybody who met Danny loved him. He and Danny had been best friends since grade school in Memphis. Danny was the reason Jack was here.

He pulled his thoughts back to the young woman across the table from him. She had the frightened, bewildered air about her that he'd seen in the faces of too many stalking victims. But underlying her fear was that core of strength that surprised and impressed him. Although he could tell she was stretched thin, she was clinging with all her might to control her life.

She wasn't going to allow the stalker to win, not if she could help it. That certainty emanated from her like a fever. He admired her for that, even while he acknowledged that her determination was going to make his job a lot harder. He'd already found out that their relationship was destined to be a battle of wills.

When he realized he was staring at her, he looked away, pulling the third note toward him. This one was the most intriguing of all.

"'Poor sweet Holly,'" he read. "'Ah but a day and the world's changed. You miss your friend and he misses you. He held this rose of love, the wasp inside and all. Fear not my dearest love. When you are ready I will be here.'"

Jack's deep voice spoke those awful words that echoed in Holly's dreams, that made her know this nightmare was real.

"Where was this one?"

Her gaze slid past him as she remembered. "It was with a stack of mail."

"In the mailbox? So it had an envelope?"

"Yes. No." She frowned. "I'm not sure." She paused. "No. It wasn't in an envelope."

Jack's nod reminded her of his certainty that the stalker had access to her home. She shuddered. Uncle Virgil was right. Jack's questions were unnerving and unnecessary. He already knew all this.

"When did you find it?"

"Four weeks ago today."

"Right about the time you announced your trip."

"You know, I didn't *announce* my trip. I'm not the town celebrity."

Jack raised that irritating brow. "Maybe not, but didn't everyone in town know you were going to Chicago for that seminar?"

She shrugged. "Probably. Living in a small town is kind of like living in a glass house."

"So your stalker knew you were leaving."

"Oh God, that's true." A shiver of revulsion skimmed down her spine. "I just want a normal life," she said sadly.

"Then, work with me. Where was this note?" He pushed it toward her.

She suppressed the urge to push away. "It wasn't with sympathy cards or wedding gifts, like the other two. There was no occasion that called for a card. It was just there."

That was the important thing. Holly understood, just as he did, the significance of the third note: there was no reason for it. It had arrived three months after Danny's death.

"Was this the first time you'd spent any time out of town in a while?"

She nodded. "With my job at the hospital and my fitness classes, plus cooking for Uncle Virgil and Aunt

Bode three nights a week, it's been two years since I've taken any time off.''

''Stalkers like to maintain a steady uninterrupted sense of control. Any break in routine, like your trip out of town, can cause severe agitation, trigger the stalker's need for attention.''

Holly's eyes widened like those of a small animal trapped by a predator. Suppressing the urge to reassure her, knowing she needed to understand just how dangerous her stalker was, Jack deliberately turned his attention back to the last note.

Thank God her great-uncle had been smart enough to bag it. Chief McCray had had the police lab in Jackson check for latent prints on all three notes, but nothing conclusive had shown up. From Jack's inspection, they looked clean, and the paper was unremarkable. It was standard copier paper. No watermark or identifiable grain.

He hoped the FBI lab could pull enough epithelial cells for a DNA match. Then all he'd have to do was line up everybody in Maze and swab them for DNA. He snorted to himself. Fat chance of that.

''So, about Detective Barbour,'' he prompted.

Holly wondered at the shadow in his expression. His mouth was set, his eyes dark. She could almost think it was sadness.

''Danny died of a wasp sting. When I saw the reference to the wasp in the note, it really spooked me. I thought someone had a sick sense of humor.''

''Everything the stalker does is deliberate. Danny's death was no accident. Nor was the note. There was a lethal concentration of venom in his system, many times the amount in a single wasp sting.''

''Oh, no.'' Holly absorbed this new, horrific information. Her heart beat painfully in her chest and her throat felt clogged with tears. "So Danny was murdered, too—" Her voice broke. "But why? It doesn't make any sense to kill Danny."

Jack's face was inscrutable. "There are only two explanations for why the killer targeted Danny."

Holly waited, dreading the words he was about to say, hating the fact that she already knew them.

"Either because you and Danny were becoming too intimate, or because Danny had discovered the killer's identity."

She wanted to clamp her palms over her ears and pretend she didn't know that Danny had died because of his association with her. "We weren't intimate."

"Tell me about the day he died."

"He was invited to Uncle Virgil's for dinner that night," she said shakily. Her throat tightened and the dull pain behind her right eye became sharper. She rubbed her temple.

"When he didn't answer his home phone or his cell, Uncle Virgil sent the officers on duty to his apartment and...found him—" Her voice gave out.

"He was dead."

She nodded, the sad, lost look shadowing her face.

Jack's heart twisted in compassion for her. He'd always hated this part of his job. This mining of people's memories in order to put together a profile of the victims. It was necessary, though, because only with a complete understanding of the victims could he come to understand the killer.

This time was doubly hard, because Holly wasn't the only one grieving for Danny Barbour. He was, too. If he'd gotten back to his friend in time, maybe Danny would still be alive.

"Danny thought the person sending the notes could have killed Brad and Ralph."

Jack knew that Danny hadn't mentioned his theory to Virgil McCray because he didn't want to alarm Holly's great-uncle unnecessarily. He'd said that on the voice-mail message he'd left for Jack while Jack was in the hospital.

"Danny said the person believed only I would understand his messages. He said obsessed admirers build up a fantasy in their mind, thinking they have a relationship when there isn't one. But why didn't the third note come in March, when Danny died, instead of three months later?"

Jack agreed. That was the question. The third note was different, out of place, out of time.

Holly groped for a chair and sat down. "Danny always said the notes held the clues." She laughed, sounding faintly hysterical. "I guess he didn't know how right he was. Of all the detectives who have worked for Uncle Virgil, Danny was the most dedicated. It was like an obsession with him."

Jack suppressed a sad smile. Danny had always been like that, even when they were kids. He'd thrown himself into everything he did with his whole heart and soul, unlike Jack, who had spent the years after his mother's death learning how to shield his emotions behind a wall of icy reserve.

Jack wasn't sure why anyone would invest their whole heart and soul in anything. There was too much chance of being hurt.

"Jack? What about Danny's casebook? Was there anything in there that would help?"

The small, bound notebook in his jacket pocket felt as heavy as lead. He wasn't ready to reveal that Danny had been his best friend. Holly might be less inclined to trust him fully if she thought he had a personal agenda. She didn't know him, didn't understand how committed he was to separating his emotions from his job. He would never jeopardize a case that way. "I'll have to take a look at it."

"Well, do. I can't believe Uncle Virgil didn't give it to you, because Danny wrote everything in that book."

She wasn't exactly right. Danny had used his case-book to record his notes on cases, but he was very careful not to write his theories or his suspicions in it. Danny knew that notes could be entered into evidence. A good lawman kept his speculations in his head.

However, he had jotted a note to call Jack.

Jack resisted the temptation to put his hand in his pocket. "I'll check into it."

"I think it would help you a lot. Danny thought Ralph might have been drowned."

"So do I, because of the reference to water in the note. Your fiancé never arrived at the pharmacy meeting he was scheduled to attend at a restaurant overlooking the Barnett reservoir in Jackson. Detective Barbour had asked to have area lakes, including the reservoir dragged. We're going ahead with that."

Holly's wide-eyed gaze filled with sadness. "I had hoped Ralph had just gotten cold feet."

He hurt for her. He knew he was systematically destroying all the false assurances she'd gathered around herself to cushion her from the truth. As he'd told her on the plane, she did it to feel safe, but her sense of security was based on false premises, and deep down she knew it.

A deep yearning came over him to gather her close,

to shield her. But hiding behind him wouldn't make her safe. He needed her to be clear-headed, to concentrate on the facts so she could help him find the killer.

"Jack? Danny was a good cop. How could the killer have gotten close enough to kill him?"

"He died from an anaphylactic reaction to a lethal dose of wasp venom. That indicates murder at a distance. The autopsy didn't turn up an injection site. Just that one wasp sting. For the moment, we're not sure."

Holly made a little choked noise, and Jack noticed how pale she was. She massaged her neck and frowned. "I'm sorry, but I need to go home. I left my migraine tablets and I need one if I'm going to cook for Uncle Virgil and Aunt Bode this evening."

"When do you go back to work?"

"I took vacation from the hospital this week, but I have two elderly aerobics classes. My ladies are counting on me."

And he already knew enough about her to know she wouldn't let them down.

"So you didn't free up your schedule for your honeymoon?" He tossed the words out without thinking.

She glanced up, and something hot and compelling flashed between them. He felt it like a chain of fire, drawing them together, threatening to engulf them if they got too close.

After a moment Holly closed her eyes, breaking the spell. She rubbed her temple. "Somehow I guessed this marriage wouldn't include a honeymoon."

THEY DROVE SILENTLY through the quiet tree-lined streets of Maze in Holly's car. Jack noticed that everybody craned their necks and stared as they drove by. *Small towns.*

He knew he stuck out like a sore thumb. Not only because he'd presumed to show up unannounced, married to one of theirs, but also because he had no idea how small towns worked. He'd grown up in Memphis, then moved to Washington D.C. as soon as he turned eighteen. He qualified for an academic scholarship, and when he graduated he applied for a job with the FBI. His job was his life.

His home life had been just him and his mother and her constant stream of boyfriends. He hardly remembered his father, who had died when he was five. He'd loved his mother, tried to protect her, but he'd been too young, too small. He had no experience with the kind of family and friends Holly had.

And he certainly had never lived with a woman before. He was the quintessential fish out of water.

He wished he could use the fact that everybody knew everybody else in this town to his advantage. He glanced over at Holly. He was counting on the townspeople accepting him because she had married him, and using that acceptance to observe and catalog their behavior.

Would it take much to form an obsession with her? He didn't think so. She was lovely and caring. It wasn't hard to understand how she would attract an erotomaniac, the type of delusional psychopath who believed that he was in a relationship with the target. All it would take was a smile and a kind word to have him believing she loved him.

Jack had never had a case quite like this one. Most of his stalking cases had involved domestic violence. Too often, the locals didn't call in the Division until the victim or someone she cared about had been murdered by her stalker. And in almost one hundred percent of cases, the victim had known the man who killed her. He'd only worked a few cases where the stalker was unknown—mostly celebrity stalkings.

He'd occasionally gone undercover as an employee or a relative, but he'd never posed as a victim's husband, living in the same house, sleeping in the same bed.

So much about this case was different. Usually if he had a live vic, she cowered helplessly, not really believing anyone could stop the nightmare. Her innocence and trust were already gone. Holly still clung to hers with a ferocity that amazed him.

As he pulled into Holly's driveway, his cell phone rang. Holly opened the passenger door, but he motioned for her to sit still.

"Hey, Ice Man."

"Nat." His pulse sped up at the sound of the Division's computer expert's low-pitched voice. She'd only call for one reason. She had the background checks for Hanks and Winger. "Thanks for the quick turnaround. I know you're working several cases."

"Anything for you, darlin'." Natasha Rudolph's sultry voice was as exotic as her appearance. She was tall, blond, with eyes so dark blue they were almost black.

He snorted. "Right. So, what have you got?"

"Stanley Hanks did a nickel in the state penitentiary for armed robbery of a liquor store when he was eighteen."

"What about Winger?"

"Robert Winger has been picked up a few times for domestic disturbance. Seems he has a temper. Of course, lucky for him, he also has a mother who would do anything for her little boy. Two of the three incidents were against her, and she refused to file charges. The third was in a public place, against a man he was apparently having dinner with, who also refused to file charges.''

Jack glanced at Holly. ''Domestic disturbances. Thanks, Nat. This helps a lot.''

''You sure found a little hotbed of intrigue down there in Mississippi, didn't you.''

Jack laughed shortly. ''Small towns.'' He turned off the phone and got out of the car, going around to open the door for Holly. She opened it herself and waved him away.

''I'm okay,'' she said softly, shading her eyes. ''It's just that these headaches make my eyes sensitive to sunlight. What was that all about on the phone?''

Jack explained as he took her arm to help her inside. She looked as if she was in a lot of pain. He checked the street. It appeared quiet and calm, a peaceful southern street in a peaceful southern town.

They walked in through the garage.

Jack's gaze automatically swept the kitchen as he headed to the sink and grabbed a glass. ''You go get your medication. I'll bring you some water.''

She walked through to the living room. ''Now what?''

The odd note in her voice instantly warned him that something was wrong. ''What is it?'' He stepped through the kitchen door in time to see her bending down to pick something up.

''Stop!'' he ordered sharply.

Holly jumped, but to her credit, she froze in place, awkwardly bent. ''Jack. It's just a book.''

''Quiet.'' He stood perfectly still, balanced on the balls of his feet, one hand out in a warning gesture.

He listened. There was no sound but their breathing. He berated himself for letting down his guard. He'd let the fact that Holly was in pain and needed medication distract him from doing his job. He should have done his usual sweep of every room. *He* should have found the book.

He looked at its position, lying open on the floor, then at the front door, the windows, the hardwood floors. Everything looked undisturbed, even the shelf above the book. There was no sign that anyone had been there.

"Can I move now? I'm going to throw up if I don't get something for this headache."

She did look as if she might faint at any moment. He nodded curtly. "Slowly back away the way you came. Try not to disturb anything. There may be some hairs or fibers."

Her heart pounding, Holly straightened cautiously and took a step backward.

Still poised like a tiger ready to spring, Jack pulled a pair of latex gloves and a small high-powered flashlight from his pocket. He pulled on the gloves, then carefully examined the floor with the flashlight.

Holly watched him with interest, trying to ignore the pain in her head. He was looking for evidence, she presumed. Finally, he moved slowly toward the fallen book.

"Do you recognize the book?"

Holly started to move closer, but he held up a hand. "From there."

"No. It looks like a textbook."

He stopped directly above the book, and scrutinized the shelves. "It didn't come from these shelves." He bent his knees until he was sitting on his haunches.

Then he scanned the open pages, his silky black hair sliding over his forehead.

"So someone brought it into my house and put it there," she said, unnerved by his careful, methodical caution.

To her dismay, he uttered a curse under his breath. His jaw was clenched in concentration.

Holly gazed at the book on the floor as if it were an exposed land mine. Her feet tingled with the impulse to run away. But even stronger was the need to know what her stalker had left her.

"What does it say?"

Jack didn't look up.

"Come on, Jack. He left it in my house. I have a right to know. Tell me, or I'll come over there and read it myself."

Jack sighed. "One passage is marked. It says, 'I struck him, he groveled of course— For, what was his force? I pinned him to earth with my weight.'"

"Oh my God," she whispered.

The stalker had sent her a warning. He was coming after Jack.

Chapter Five

The killer had made his presence known. This time he wasn't content to leave a subtle note where it might be found. He'd boldly entered Holly's home in broad daylight.

Jack mentioned none of this to Holly as he tucked her in bed. Her migraine had hit her full force. He felt unexpectedly helpless as he brought her migraine tablets to her, then left her to rest.

He retrieved his portable evidence kit and returned to the living room to finish processing the crime scene. The infrequent times he got to go over a fresh crime scene, he liked doing it alone, without distractions.

And Holly Frasier could definitely be termed a distraction.

With his Polaroid camera, he took double pictures of the room, the book lying open on the floor, the undisturbed shelves above. He wanted a set to send to the lab at Headquarters and a set to keep.

With a sable brush, he dusted the inside doorknob for prints. He'd like to dust the outer knob but he couldn't take a chance on the neighbors, or the killer, seeing him acting like a cop. Maybe after dark he could do it while pretending to change the porch lightbulb.

As he expected, the inside knob had been wiped clean. There weren't any prints at all, not even the usual smudges that any surface in a house picks up. Whoever the guy was, he was careful. He didn't want to be caught.

Jack thought about the preliminary profile he and Eric had put together. Typically, stalkers were one of three types: erotomanic stalkers, revenge stalkers or intimate partner stalkers. The first type built an entire fantasy relationship on a smile or a kind word. The second were usually more dangerous, perceiving some wrong, and out to take revenge on their imagined persecutor. The third type was typically the most deadly—the rejected lover, often from an abusive relationship. Still, the erotomaniac could be capable of violence, especially against those he perceived as barriers to the object of his obsession.

Jack had the impression that Eric was puzzled by the notes. This UnSub exhibited characteristics of both a serial killer and a stalker. That alone made him an enigma. Serial killers took pride in staying one step ahead of the authorities. Stalkers rarely bothered to hide their actions.

Most victims of erotomanic stalkers were all too aware of their admirer—receiving gifts or phone calls, seeing them everywhere. Many times the victims moved or even took on new identities to escape. The polar opposite was the hidden stalker, more dangerous because he stalked in silence. The victim might not know about him until it was too late.

Jack had encountered every type.

He pressed a special gelatin lifting substance along

the curve of the brass doorknob, then placed it carefully back in its container. If there were any marks or irregularities on the knob, the gel would pick it up.

He copied the phrase from the open page of the high school English textbook into his notebook, then took a close-up shot of the pages before he closed the book and bagged it. On the front of the bag he wrote the page numbers and then filled out the request form. The lab would test the outer surface and the pages for epithelial DNA and prints.

With a magnifying glass and his flashlight, he went over the hardwood floor more carefully. No hairs. No fibers. There was a fine patina of dust on the wood. The only disturbance was a smear along one plank. He took two pictures.

As Jack pressed a strip of lift tape along the thin smear of dust to lift and preserve its pattern, a pair of small bare feet with pink painted toes appeared in his peripheral vision. His body tightened with desire.

"Did you find any evidence? Did the book have a name in it?" Holly asked.

He shook his head and peeled the tape carefully. "It's a high school English lit text. There's not much here. That's not unusual, though." He applied the tape to an acid-free backing card. "Most evidence is identified in the crime lab, not at the scene."

"Are you taking all that to Uncle Virgil this evening?"

"No, I usually either deliver it to a contact or mail it back to Headquarters. I'll probably mail this. I don't want anyone here to associate me with law enforcement. If your stalker becomes suspicious that I'm anything other than your husband, he could go to ground, and it might be months before he surfaces again."

He didn't tell her there was another possibility. That the stalker could become enraged that Holly had betrayed him—and come after her.

Neither option was acceptable.

He rose, rolling up the paper with the tape on it, and looked at her.

The sight of her stunned him. She had twisted her hair up and caught it carelessly with a barrette, and strands were escaping everywhere. One cheek was pink where she'd lain against a pillow, and her eyes were dreamy with sleep or with the drug she'd taken for her headache.

No one could deny that she was reasonably pretty and had a dynamite body, but right now, with her eyes shining, her lips moist and her hair sexily tousled, she was irresistibly beautiful.

"Don't stare at me," she said. "I've been asleep. I'll look presentable in a few minutes."

"You look presentable now."

She blinked and a tiny gasp escaped her lips.

Damn. He shouldn't have said that, shouldn't even be thinking it. He'd been caught off guard by her drowsy loveliness, and it was playing havoc with his usual careful detachment. Irritated at himself, Jack took it out on her.

"Listen to me, Holly. We're supposed to be married. Until this is over, I'm your husband, saying things a husband would say to his wife. As I told you yesterday, even our movements inside these walls must convey, to anyone who happens by, that we're newlyweds. You need to wipe the term *FBI* out of your brain. You need to get into the role you're playing. Think of yourself as my wife, 24/7. We're in a play and you and I are the stars. You're center stage at all times. If you forget that, the consequences could be deadly. Got it?''

Her throat moved as she swallowed. For a second he was afraid her composure would crumble. Reluctantly, hyper-aware of the new, disturbing feelings she evoked in him, he reached out and caught a fallen strand of hair, his fingers brushing her soft cheek. He couldn't let anything happen to her. He had to act like her husband, although it would make his life much less complicated if he could maintain his distance, physically and emotionally.

"You asked me not to patronize you. I'm asking you to work with me here.''

She nodded, hugging herself. "I understand. I'm just scared. You can't imagine what it's like for me to live like this, knowing someone is out there, threatening the people I care about.''

Jack's jaw tightened until it ached as he tried to suppress the vision of his mother, lying so still, his stepfather's brutal fingerprints outlined in bruises around her throat.

"I don't have to imagine,'' he said harshly, then winced, regretting his revealing words. He quickly covered. "I see it every day in my work. I'm more interested in keeping you alive.''

He took a deep breath. "Now I have to ask you some questions.''

"Do you mind if I get a glass of water and sit down? I'm still a little woozy from the headache medicine.''

He followed her into the kitchen.

"Did you know Stanley Hanks had been in prison?''

Her chin went up a fraction. "Of course. He got in trouble right after the senior prom. He robbed a liquor store with his dad's gun and went to Parchman, for five years or so.''

"Why didn't you mention that when we were talking about him?'' He filled a glass with water and handed it to her.

She shrugged. "I guess I thought you already knew. You seem to know everything else.''

"How about Winger's domestic disputes?''

"Domestic disputes? You're talking about the couple of times the neighbors have complained about Bob yelling?''

"Yelling and more, from the reports.''

She drank the water. "I told you, Bob has problems. His mother is manipulative and demanding. Sometimes he loses control. He's very...conflicted.''

"Conflicted enough to become obsessed with a nice young woman who will listen to him whine about his life?''

Holly frowned and rubbed her temple. "I can't imagine Bob being violent, but from what you say, I guess it could be him.'' A shudder rippled through her.

"Those two aren't the only interesting guys on your list of names, either. Donald Sheffield is under a restraining order for getting physical with a girlfriend in Jackson. And did you know that Ralph Peyton had taken out a large insurance policy with you as beneficiary?''

"What?'' Holly's eyes widened in genuine shock. "Why didn't he tell me?''

"Maybe he intended to. Your boyfriend Isley wrote that policy as well as your husband's life insurance policy.''

"Earl? Is that significant? There's only one other insurance agent in town."

"It could be."

WHEN HOLLY CAME OUT of her room an hour later, dressed in a soft linen dress and backless sandals, Jack was waiting. As usual, he looked crisp and cool, even in jeans. His hair was slightly damp from his shower and his face was freshly shaved.

Think of him as her husband? She almost gulped. That was not going to be a problem. Her problem was she didn't have to act like she was attracted to him. She *was* attracted to him.

And it wasn't just because of his dark good looks. It was his strength, his attentiveness to her needs, his occasional tender gestures that drew her to him.

But she had to be careful. He was here to do a job. When it was over he'd go back to his life and she'd go back to hers. She didn't like the empty feeling that thought gave her.

He turned around to pick up the box he'd packed and she saw the gun holstered at the small of his back. The sight of the cold steel magnified the seriousness of their situation.

He glanced up as he clipped his cell phone onto his belt. "Something wrong?" he asked.

"Are you going to carry that thing everywhere?"

"My weapon? Yes."

"How will you keep people from—"

He grabbed a lightweight jacket from the back of a chair and put it on, settling it onto his shoulders with a sexy, masculine shrug.

Even the awareness of the weapon he carried didn't detract from his appeal. If anything, it made him even more dangerously sexy. She swallowed. *Not a problem.*

He smiled at her, a twinkle in his eye. "The jacket hides it. Kind of gets in the way of the husband thing, I know. But that's just something you're going to have to live with, *honey.*"

His words and his devilish smile irritated her. "Are you ready?"

"Let's go."

She gave him directions to the post office.

"How are you going to mail that to the FBI? The postmaster is an awful old gossip."

"It's addressed to my aunt Jenny at a post office box in Maryland."

"Your aunt Jenny." She marveled at the care and thought he put into every action. Considering all possibilities, thinking of every contingency.

She went in with him to mail his package.

Mr. Ames, the postmaster, eyed him like a curious bird, tilting his head and peering over his half-glasses. "So this is your new husband, Holly? What's your name, son?"

Jack glanced at Holly as he set the box down on the counter. "O'Hara. Jack O'Hara."

"Well, Jack O'Hara. You know you got the prize, don't you? We don't know what we'd do without Holly here in Maze. So you better be good to her, you understand?"

"Yes. I'm beginning to."

Mr. Ames looked at the label on the box. "Overnight, eh? So, Jack, what do you do?"

The question startled Holly. They'd never gotten around to talking about how they would field these questions. Now they were out here in the midst of the people who had known her all her life, and she had no idea how her new husband was going to respond.

Jack leaned an elbow on the counter. "I'm a writer," he said easily.

"Ah. A writer. Well, I guess that explains how you can just pick up and move down here. So what do you write?"

Holly did her best not to let her panic show. What would a real wife do? Hoping Mr. Ames wouldn't send one of his probing questions her way, she jerkily slid her arm around Jack's waist, stifling a startled yelp as her fingers touched the gun at his back.

"Honey, we're going to be late," she said, putting what she hoped was a loving tone into her voice.

"I freelance," Jack told Mr. Ames. "I was at the seminar Holly attended, doing a series of articles on strength training for a fitness magazine. Of course—" he straightened and casually put his arm around Holly's shoulder "—I have to confess, right now I'm having a little trouble concentrating. We're still honeymooning, you know."

Mr. Ames chuckled and his eyebrows went up another notch as Jack pulled Holly closer. She had the alarming notion Jack might kiss her, right here in the post office.

As Jack pressed his lips against her hair, sending shivers over her scalp, the bell on the door jangled. She pushed away and saw Bob Winger.

When he saw Holly, his face brightened like a flashlight with a new battery. "Holly, hi!"

"Hi, Bob." She looked up at Jack. "Bob, this is Jack O'Hara, my husband."

Jack held out his hand, but for a few seconds, Bob just stood there, as if stunned.

"H-husband?" he stammered. "Well, that's certainly a surprise. Um, congratulations."

"I got your phone messages, Bob," Holly said, "but I haven't had a chance to call." She felt herself blush when Jack put his arm around her shoulder as if staking his territory.

"I'm afraid I've been monopolizing her time," Jack said. "I'm sure I'll see you around, once we're more settled. Holly tells me you teach English and American literature at the high school."

Bob nodded and wiped his hand down the front of his pants.

"Sorry to run," Holly said, "but we're on our way to Uncle Virgil's house."

As they headed toward the door, Jack leaned down to whisper in her ear. "So that's Bob of the lunches that aren't dates?"

Embarrassed by his casual familiarity, she ducked out from under his arm, and almost collided with another customer.

"Excuse me— Oh!" It was Thomas Frasier, Brad's father. Holly's smile suddenly felt frozen. "Mr. Frasier, how are you?"

The older man's broad face and fair hair were just like his son's. It always pained Holly to see him—not only because of the resemblance, but also because of his undisguised hostility toward her. Thomas Frasier believed Holly had ruined his only son's promising future. He had never forgiven her for marrying Brad.

Frasier shot her a venom-laced look and pushed past her without speaking.

"Mr. Frasier." Jack's voice held the perfect note of deference. Holly cringed. Of course he knew who her ex-father-in-law was. She pushed open the exit door, but Jack didn't take the hint.

He nodded at the shorter man and held out his hand. "I'm Jack O'Hara, Holly's husband."

Brad's father looked at Jack's hand. He didn't offer his own. "I know who you are," he growled.

"Sir, I'm glad to meet you. I know you wish your son's widow well. I look forward to getting to know you and the rest of the people in Maze."

Frasier never met his gaze. He barely looked at Holly. "Better tell your new husband to watch his step around here. It's not a very friendly place for strangers."

Stepping around Jack without further acknowledgment, he approached the counter. "Ames, I've got a book I need to mail."

Holly caught Jack's eye and silently gestured with a nod. He glanced back at Thomas Frasier, then followed her out.

Relieved that Jack didn't intend to pursue his conversation with Mr. Frasier, Holly headed for the car.

Once Jack was in the driver's seat, she pleaded with him. "There are so many things you don't understand. Please don't bait Mr. Frasier. He's never gotten over Brad's death."

"Why not?"

"Are you a robot?" she cried, shocked at his response. "What kind of question is that? Because people never get over the death of a loved one. Brad was his son! He was just twenty-four. Nobody should die that young. He had his whole life ahead of him."

Jack sent her an unfathomable look. "That doesn't explain his hostility. I thought everybody in Maze adored you."

She shrugged, her heart aching. If Uncle Virgil had told Jack everything, why hadn't he told him about her and Brad? She rubbed her temple. She didn't want to talk about this.

"Holly?" Jack's voice took on a new timbre, a soothing, seductive tone. "I'm your husband. We're being watched." He put his fingers on the side of her face and urged her to look at him. "Smile for me."

She raised her gaze to his, and saw a soft, smoky concern there that sent her heart racing and lodged a lump in her throat. She gave him a tremulous smile. Then, out of the corner of her eye, she saw Brad's father glaring at them from the post office doorway, as Bob walked down the sidewalk.

Jack was just acting. She was surprised at how much that reminder hurt.

She forced her smile to stay in place, and touched his hand where it lingered on her cheek, aware that this was only the beginning of many falsely loving touches she was destined to endure before this nightmare was over.

Jack leaned over and kissed her, the hard line of his mouth softening, his lips warm, sure and slow. She closed her eyes, held captive by his mouth and the surge of need that erupted inside her. All thoughts of Brad's father flew out of her head. Her lips parted and his tongue touched hers. Then he pulled away, ducking his head briefly before he met her gaze.

The hunger was there, she was sure of it, before he morphed back into the actor playing his role.

"What's Brad's father got against you?"

"What?" she murmured, half mesmerized by his kiss and his dark gaze.

"Holly." He sounded impatient. "I'm a trained observer. I recognize hatred when I see it."

Hatred? The fantasy of yearning his kiss had stirred

waned and she was thrust back into the real world, a world where a killer was stalking her.

"Mr. Frasier blamed me for ruining Brad's pro football career. Several pro teams were watching him during his first year of college. I—thought I might be pregnant."

He sat up a little straighter and stared at her. "You were pregnant? That's not in my report."

She shook her head, remembering the mixture of joy and fear she'd felt when she looked at the little blue stick.

"We were engaged, so we just moved up the wedding date and Brad registered for the fall semester. None of the pro teams had come forward with a concrete offer anyway. But then…the pregnancy test must have been wrong."

"Or you miscarried?" His words were gentle.

She shook her head. It didn't matter now. The baby she'd wanted simply hadn't been meant to be. The tiny knot of grief and regret that lurked deep inside her throbbed painfully.

"Do you have to do this?" Her anger flared. Why was he dredging up old pain, making it new again? "Do you have to slice up every minute detail of my life like a mad scientist searching for a cancer cell?"

Jack's gaze turned cold. "Yes. I have to consider every angle. What if Brad's death *was* an accident, but his father is obsessed with making sure you can never destroy another man's life again?"

Holly stared at him. He'd voiced her own fears. She put her hand on her chest where his sharp-edged words stabbed her heart with guilt. *Never destroy another man's life.*

"You think it could be Brad's father? I thought you

said the man was an obsessed admirer. Someone who thinks I'm in love with him.''

Jack took her hand, rubbing his thumb over her knuckles. ''That's the most likely scenario, but it's not impossible that this is motivated by revenge.'' Jack pulled up to a stop sign. ''Whoever it is, I'm going to do my best to get him. Now, before we run into anyone else, let's talk about how we met and what I do for a living.''

Holly pulled her hand away, unable to bear his touch right then. He was methodically cataloging everyone in her hometown and categorizing them by the likelihood that they could be the killer. ''You just tell me what you want me to know. I can't even think right now.''

''Why don't we start with directions to your uncle's house? Do I keep going straight?''

She sat up and looked out the window, glad to have something mundane to focus on. ''Another block, and turn right at the Baptist church.''

As Jack made the turn, Holly saw the Baptist preacher, Gil Mason, out pruning the shrubs by the church. When he looked up and waved, she waved back.

''We've only known each other a couple of weeks, right? So no one will expect us to know too much about each other.''

Holly shook her head. ''We're in the Deep South, Jack. People will ask about your family history before they ask your name. So, have you ever actually done any freelance writing?''

''No.''

''Do you really have an aunt in Maryland?''

''No.''

She sighed at his monosyllabic answers. "Okay, why don't you give me the sound-bite version of your life."

Jack handled the car easily and efficiently, his large, elegant hands lightly caressing the wheel. "I'm thirty-three. Live in Chicago. Never married before. I freelance while I'm working on my novel. I'm a good cook and a better lover, and once I saw you at the fitness seminar I couldn't let you out of my sight."

"Oh, dear," Holly groaned, feeling her face heat up at his words. At least he was concise, and thorough. Although adding that "better lover" remark was just mean. She tried to banish the memory of the vision that had greeted her upon waking this morning. Jack lying in her bed, draped in her new white sheets.

She swallowed hard as they approached Uncle Virgil's house. "Here we are. It's the white house with the blue shutters."

There were three or four neighbors outside, watering their lawns, walking their dogs, or just sitting on their front porch watching traffic go by. Holly waved at each of them, feeling their curious glances like little crawly things on her skin.

Jack pulled into the driveway and grinned at her. "Is that enough information for a start?"

She looked at him and her heart fluttered in her breast. She tried to tell herself it was because of his embarrassing words, not the disarming grin that transformed his face and made him look impossibly handsome. "I can't tell anybody that."

"Maybe not, but you'll think it every time someone asks you about me. And that pretty pink blush will be worth more than a thousand words."

Holly groaned, knowing he was right. "I don't blu—"

Jack's hand came around her neck and he kissed her. This time it wasn't a sweet, comforting kiss. This kiss was hot, hard and intimate. His lips covered hers and his tongue teased her mouth open before she had a chance to react.

Holly forgot to breathe. His thumb caressed the skin just below her ear and she felt it all the way through her. All her fears, all her worries, melted beneath the strong assurance of his kiss. No one had ever taken such utter and complete control of her senses. His breathing grew rapid and ragged as her heart pounded and desire surged through her like summer lightning.

Just as she lifted her head and leaned toward him, craving more, he pulled away, leaving her half stunned. His eyes were stormy and troubled as he straightened and removed his hand from her neck.

"There," he said hoarsely. "That should stir some gossip. Now, let's go meet your family."

Chapter Six

Holly's great-aunt Bode was having a bad day. She hadn't been the same since her stroke. She sat in her rocking chair and hummed, her toneless serenade punctuated by wracking coughs. Her faded blue eyes stared vacantly. Her salt-and-pepper hair was messy and tangled, and her dress had food stains down the front.

Uncle Virgil looked haggard as he took the teakettle off the stove. "Come on in, Holly, Jack," he said, retrieving a box of tea bags from the cabinet. "Holly, come make the tea. You know the right amount of sugar to put in it."

"Okay. Hi, Aunt Bode." Holly kissed the paper-thin skin of her aunt's cheek, then walked over to the kitchen area. "Didn't the home attendant show up?"

Uncle Virgil shook his head. "I wish you'd call them for me. Bode doesn't like this new woman."

Holly wondered how many times the home attendant hadn't shown up during the two weeks she'd been gone to the seminar. Why hadn't Debi done anything? She sighed quietly. "Okay. I'll call first thing in the morning. Where's Debi?"

"Debi's right here." Her sister's voice sounded strained behind her. "But not for long."

Debi was dressed in a short leather skirt and a one-shouldered tank top. Her long bare legs were accentuated by high-heeled slides. She looked dangerously lovely, as only a tall, vital young woman can.

"Where are you going?" Holly asked as she unpinned Aunt Bode's hair and began to brush it, trying to suppress her frustration that Debi had let their great-aunt sit all day with messy hair and food-stained clothes.

"Out." The single word was a challenge.

Holly saw Jack studying Debi, his face typically expressionless but his eyes full of interest.

Holly set the hairbrush down as Debi swung open the front door. "I'll be right back," she said to Jack and Uncle Virgil, and followed Debi out onto the porch.

"What have you been doing all day? Aunt Bode's hair hasn't even been brushed."

Debi stopped halfway down the front steps and turned back. "What have I been doing? Chasing around after her, trying to keep her from hurting herself. You want to know why the home attendant didn't show? Because Aunt Bode has decided she likes to throw food at people. What have you been doing all day, Miss Newlywed? Of course, I'm sure I know the answer to that."

Holly cringed at the acid in her sister's voice. She tried to curb her impatience, but too much had happened in the past twenty-four hours and her nerves were shot.

"You don't know nearly as much as you think you do, Debi. Is it too much to ask for you to help with

Aunt Bode? You're living here rent-free. You're not working. I cook dinner over here at least three nights a week. It would be different if you were in school, but apparently you've decided not to finish your degree.''

Debi propped her fists on her hips. "You don't know what I've decided. Registration isn't over yet. I haven't made up my mind. But what are you going to do about Aunt Bode if I do go back to school? She needs to be in a home. I'm sure not going to spend my life waiting on her and Uncle Virgil. I'm not like you. I don't feel the need to jump every time they even look like they need something. Of course, now that you've set up housekeeping with your hunky stranger of a husband you'll probably end up leaving this one-horse town. Then what will I do?"

Debi was really upset. Her eyes were bright with tears, her body stiff and straight, with her fists clenched at her sides, just like when she was a child.

Holly's heart softened at Debi's vulnerability. "Debi, honey, I'm not planning to go away. Where did all this come from?"

"Maybe it comes from me being afraid you've lost your mind. Where did *he* come from?"

Holly swallowed, wondering how to answer Debi's question. She'd never lied to her little sister before.

"Jack O'Hara is no hometown boy, Hol. I don't know where you found him or what possessed you to actually marry him, but he's too sharp. Too intense. He'll never live here. He'll take you away." She stopped, and tears glimmered in her eyes. She held up her hands. "Never mind. It's your life. I don't have any right—"

"Debi, come on. You're my sister. I love you."

Holly smiled and held out her arms. "It's always been you and me, kid." Debi might be a couple of inches taller than Holly, but she would always be her baby sister.

Debi backed away. "I've gotta go. I've got people waiting for me."

Holly felt her sister's rejection like a physical blow to her stomach. Debi had never refused a hug before. Holly took a step forward. "Debi, we need to talk about this. There's more to it than you know."

Debi folded her arms and sighed, putting on a sulky, impatient expression, and Holly knew from experience that her sister had stopped listening.

"Okay, go on. We'll talk later. But try not to be too late getting back. You know how Uncle Virgil worries."

"Trust me, I know. When will everyone accept that I'm an adult? I don't need people telling me what to do. You should be grateful I'm staying here so you can play house with your hunky new husband."

Holly flinched. Debi was feeling like Holly had abandoned her. She needed to know the truth. When they got home, she'd ask Jack about letting Debi in on their secret, that they were married in name only. That as soon as the stalker was caught, Jack would go on to his next case, and Holly would still be there to take care of everything.

The thought didn't cheer Holly as she stood on the porch listening to the crickets and frogs after Debi's Firebird sped away.

Farther down the street she heard another car engine flare to life and roar away, but when she looked, she didn't see anything but a small cloud of dust.

The front screen door squeaked, and Holly knew

without looking that Jack was behind her. How could she tell? She took a long breath. It was some combination of scent, sound, and an aura that emanated from him. Soap and outdoors and the soft swish of cotton and calm strength.

"Are you okay?" he whispered, his voice closer than she'd expected. If she leaned back an inch, she could rest against him. She stiffened.

It occurred to her that although she'd never spent a lot of time regretting what might have been or yearning for what might be, she'd already gotten used to having Jack there to lean on, to depend on. What would it be like to know he'd always be there?

"Debi thinks you're taking me away from her," she said, trying to sound light, but failing.

"Yeah, I heard. How did she act when you married Brad?"

"She was eleven when I left for college. You'd have thought I died, the way she cried herself sick." Holly hugged herself. "That was the age I was when our parents died. I think I know how she felt." A lump grew in her throat. "Maybe she's right. Maybe I am trying to get away."

To her surprise, Jack slipped his arms around her waist. "What are you doing?" she whispered, dismayed at how easily his touch could banish her worries and make her feel safe.

"I'm comforting my wife. A good husband knows when his wife needs support."

His breath tickled her ear. She shivered as a deep thrill spun through her.

"Is Debi always so volatile?"

"Volatile?" That was a good word for Debi. "You could say that," she breathed, wondering if the neighbors were watching, amazed at how much she hoped they were, if it gave her an excuse to accept Jack's embrace.

She continued talking because it kept her focused on something aside from his warm, hard body against her. "Debi was so young. She looked to me to take care of her."

"To you? You were a child, too. What about your aunt and uncle?"

"Uncle Virgil has been a policeman his whole life. Aunt Bode's always been eccentric. She was fun, except when she'd get into one of her moods, but she was never very motherly. She didn't quite know what to do with two little girls."

His fingers tightened and he pulled her closer.

"What about the car?" he asked with his typical single-minded focus.

But his practical words were at odds with his low, seductive voice, and his lips moving against her skin nearly caused her knees to buckle.

She struggled to concentrate. "The second one?" She angled her head away from his mouth, which was brushing her earlobe with disastrous effects on her ability to think.

"Mmm-hmm." Jack took full advantage of her exposed neck and pushed her hair away with his hand as his tongue lightly touched the surprisingly sensitive place just behind her ear.

Her thighs tightened as her body reacted.

Lord, nobody had ever kissed her precisely there before. She had no idea that the delicate skin behind her ear could be so erotic.

For a few seconds, she was lost in sensation. She leaned back, only to come up against a shocking hardness pressing against her backside. He was aroused, too. A sense of power and satisfaction swirled through her. Jack O'Hara, for all his professional detachment, wanted her.

His arm tightened around her waist as he wound strands of her hair between his fingers and pulled her head back to press kisses along her jaw. He shifted, widening his stance, pulling her up close against his arousal.

"Holly, the car?"

His words finally sunk in, and she remembered that all this was an act.

He was just doing his job. She was his assignment. His being affected by her was nothing more than a man's physical reaction to a woman.

"I heard it start up but I didn't see anything," she said tightly, pulling away from his touch, embarrassed that she'd let herself respond to him, even for a moment. He let her go.

A disturbing thought occurred to her as she turned around. "It was him, wasn't it?"

To her consternation, he reached out and touched her cheek. Her response was instantaneous, an aftershock of the desire that had rocked her just a few moments before. So what if this was just a job to him. She wanted to know more about him, and about herself. She wanted to feel his hands against her bare skin, wanted to feel him cup her breasts, trace her waist and hips, touch her in places that hadn't been touched in a long, long time.

"I'm going to take a look around. You didn't see the color, the make, anything?" He met her gaze, his eyes frosty, his manner back to the consummate professional.

Hurt and embarrassed, Holly couldn't do anything but shake her head.

Jack flashed a quick grin that didn't reach his eyes. "I'll be right back to give you a hand with dinner. I've got a trick or two I can do with chicken that only takes about a half hour."

Holly nodded jerkily, feeling like a child who'd been scolded. She took a second to compose her face, then went inside.

JACK STOOD ON THE PORCH cursing himself for reacting sexually to Holly. He was finding it harder and harder to control his growing desire for her.

He was no stranger to undercover work. He was used to setting himself up as bait. But not for one instant had he forgotten his primary goal—to free the victim or the victim's family from their terror.

He'd only been with Holly one day and he'd already nearly gotten lost in her fascinating contradictions. She was strong but vulnerable. Rational and intelligent, but innocent. She was his assignment, but she was fast becoming more than just a victim who needed his protection. He twisted the gold band on his finger. Why was he having so much trouble staying detached?

He took a long, cleansing breath. The air didn't smell quite as good since she'd gone inside. The taste of her skin lingered on his tongue.

He clamped his teeth and slapped his palm against the porch rail, hoping the sting of the blow would knock away the sweet, sharp memory of her firm backside pressed intimately against him. He had to keep a clear head, and for the first time in his career, he was finding it difficult.

He'd never been anything other than completely

professional in his relationships with victims. Caring, yes. Protective, certainly. But after the assignment was over, he'd always been able to walk away, knowing he'd done his best.

But Holly had knocked his orderly world out of balance. He found himself struggling with inappropriate desires. And feelings and thoughts were clawing their way to the surface of his consciousness for the first time in over twenty years. He didn't like any of it.

He steeled himself as memories washed over him in colors of dark red and black and bright, bright light. His stepfather, raging drunk and defying his mother's restraining order; himself too young, too weak, only half conscious after his stepfather's offhand blow.

His mother screaming, then still. So very still.

He cocked his fist and aimed it at the porch rail, then lowered his arm and walked deliberately down the steps. It wouldn't do any good to batter Virgil's porch.

He'd spent twenty years putting all that fear and anger to positive use. Enduring his mother's murder and testifying against his stepfather had taught Jack a number of things.

Emotions got in the way. Calm, icy detachment made it possible to bear anything. And putting away other scum like his stepfather was what he wanted to do with his life.

The sun was low in the sky as he walked down the sidewalk to the street, pulling his cell phone from his pocket.

He was glad he'd unabashedly eavesdropped on Holly's conversation with her sister. He wasn't sure yet if Holly would have mentioned the second car. But the idea that someone was furtively parked near Virgil's house could be vitally important.

Holly had told Winger they were coming over to Virgil's tonight.

Jack thought back to the drive over here. He was certain no one had followed them. Holly had told him she generally cooked dinner for her aunt and uncle three nights a week, so he was sure the stalker knew her routine.

Several streetlights were broken, littering the ground with bits of glass. Maybe kids playing with rocks. Maybe someone wanting the cover of darkness.

He toyed with his cell phone as he took in every inch of the area. Not far from where he stood, he saw a dark smear on the curb. Had the unknown car parked too close and scraped its tires?

Pulling out a small envelope and his pocketknife, he glanced up and down the street, but didn't see anyone. Quickly, he dropped to his haunches and scraped some rubber into the bag. He wasn't sure this rubber was from the suspicious car, but he was taking no chances. He never did.

He owed a debt to Danny, his friend, who had trusted him. Today, twenty years after the first person he'd loved had been killed, he had experience, strength, and the power of the FBI behind him.

He wasn't about to let this killer win.

Straightening, he checked again to be sure no one was watching. He considered the little street with its quaint houses and perfect lawns. It was one of the maze of quiet streets that made up this town, so aptly named Maze. No blaring music, no bright flicker of cigarette lighters or kids hanging out on porch steps, with nothing to do but get into trouble. Just the smell of fried chicken and coffee and the sound of crickets chirping.

Somehow irritated, and missing the impersonal bustle of D.C., Jack walked back toward the house and dialed the Division's profiler.

"Yeah?" Eric's familiar voice sounded distracted.

"Baldwyn? You're answering your phone?" There was a joke around the office that paying for a phone for Eric Baldwyn was a waste of money. When the Division's profiler was working on a case he rarely spoke to anyone, even in person, and he never answered the phone. Jack had planned to leave him a voice-mail message.

"Very funny, Ice Man. How's married life?"

"Did Decker tell you to say that?" Jack sat down on the porch steps and leaned back against the rail.

"No, why?"

"Never mind." He shot a quick glance toward the screen door. He could hear Holly's musical voice and Virgil's rumbling answers floating out from the house. "What have you got on the items that have gone missing from Holly's house?"

"Your UnSub is a collector," Eric said patiently. "You'll probably find a shrine to her when you find him."

"Yeah. That's what I figured. But usually they keep photographs, newspaper clippings. Stuff collected at a distance."

"Right. This guy is either arrogant or desperate to risk exposure by entering her house. You didn't include the exact date or time any of the items disappeared."

"Don't know that. But here's a flash. Today an English lit textbook was left on her floor, open to a passage by Browning.''

''Today?''

''Yep. It was a message for me. I'm sending the book and some photos to the lab.''

''So, he knows you're there, and you've rattled him. Likely suspects?''

''Just everyone in town—and no one in particular.''

Eric made an impatient sound.

''I'm serious. Everybody in town knows her, cares about her. I've only met a few people but I've been threatened by every one of them.''

''Threatened?''

''Never mind. Bad joke. Every male in town has this 'you better be good to her or you'll answer to me' attitude.'' Jack arched his shoulder, which had started to ache, and switched the phone to his other hand, checking one more time that nobody was listening at the door or lurking around the yard.

''Okay, assuming most of them are just concerned friends, who does bother you?''

''Nat ran a list of boyfriends for me. There are several possibles on it. And I've got the dead husband's father, who blames her for ruining his son's career. The son gave up a pro football slot to marry her. Then there's a big chunk of policeman who acts like it would be his personal pleasure to take me apart if I let Holly break a fingernail.''

Jack paused as a car drove by. He raised his hand in a casual wave. ''Think it could be the father-in-law? Motivated by revenge?''

''Making the assumption that the husband's death was an accident?'' There was a long silence. Jack waited. He knew Eric worked intuitively. He seemed to have an empathic link with victims. Finally the younger man spoke.

"The father-in-law could be a candidate for a revenge-motivated stalking. But…" Eric paused for so long that Jack started to fidget.

"The UnSub went into her house in broad daylight?"

"Yep."

"I assume she lives in a close-knit neighborhood? Probably knows everyone and everyone knows her?"

"You got it."

"And even though she knows everybody in town, she doesn't leave her house unlocked. The missing articles and the coincidences of the deaths were already getting to her, but she defends anyone you ask about?"

Jack sat up. Eric's intuition was kicking in. He had Holly described perfectly. "That's my girl," he said wryly.

"So she's started to act differently. That plus your presence has agitated the UnSub, which is why he has already acted outside of his usual pattern by taking the chance of entering her house in broad daylight to leave the book there."

"Exactly."

"He's escalating." Eric drew in a swift breath. "I don't think the husband's death was an accident," he said, his voice muffled as if he were wiping his face. "I don't feel revenge."

Jack stood and paced the sidewalk. He knew Eric was the best, but he didn't understand the profiler's *feelings*. He listened to the facts, but then he just sort of *felt* something. The thing that most bothered Jack was how often Eric's feelings were right.

"I still think it's an erotomaniac. You're in the

house, right? As far as everyone knows, you two are married?''

''Right.''

''I mean *married*. As in, if someone walked in unannounced or looked in the window, you would still look married.''

Jack swallowed, recalling Holly's soft breathing in the night. His thumb touched the wedding band. ''Yeah. Mostly.''

''If you've fooled him, if he knows that behind those doors you're really intimate, I believe he'll continue to escalate and probably get careless. Are you?''

Jack raked fingers through his hair, stood, and began pacing the sidewalk. Eric's matter-of-fact questions were making him squirm. ''Are we what?'' he parried.

''You want it in four-letter words? Intimate.''

Jack snorted. ''Of course not. I'm on a job, Baldwyn. It's not necessary.''

''I wouldn't be too sure about that. Correct me if I'm wrong, but isn't this a unique situation for you? You've never had an Unknown Subject with both stalker and serial-killer characteristics and a live victim at precisely the same time, have you?''

Jack didn't answer. Eric was right. In his previous cases, either the victim knew her stalker all too well, or the stalker had already turned violent and the vic was dead.

''So, you don't know who the stalker is, where he is, how closely he watches her or her house. You can tell, you know.''

''Tell what?''

''When two people are in an intimate relationship. If your stalker is obsessed with your vic, he'll be attuned to every breath she takes. He'll know if she's—"

"Crap, Baldwyn. Are you deliberately screwing with my head?"

"Not at all. Come on, Ice Man. Anything to catch the killer, right?"

"I'll make it work," he said hoarsely, as an unwanted vision rose in his brain: Holly's hair spread across his pillow and her perfect breasts bared to his touch.

"What about the items the UnSub chose? What's he going to go after next?"

"I've studied the list. It's obvious he's preparing a place for them to be together. A love nest."

The words hit Jack like a punch to the stomach. He'd expected Eric to say exactly that, so why the instantaneous adrenaline reaction? Why the barely controllable urge to break something?

"What?" He'd missed Eric's last remark.

"I said, I'd expect something virginal, but he's already got that white nightgown. So maybe symbolic of a wedding? A bridal veil or gown? Or if nothing else, her wedding pictures with the dead husband cut out."

Apprehension sliced through Jack. "You think he's escalating that fast?"

"You showing up unexpectedly married to her may have disrupted his plans by a year or more. He could strike at any time."

Jack rubbed his jaw. "Good. Do me a favor will you? Tell Nat to check Theodore 'T-Bone' Polk."

"T-Bone?" Eric sounded amused.

"Jack?" It was Holly, calling his name through the screen door.

He froze. "Yeah. Tell Nat to run him. I'll talk to you later, kid." He pocketed his phone.

"Ready to start dinner?" he said, trying for casual but coming off hard.

Holly stood haloed by the light from the kitchen. Jack couldn't take his eyes off her. The backlighting accentuated her slim, toned body. The ache of desire that hadn't gone away since their encounter on the porch flared, fueled by Eric's words.

"Well, around here, unless you dress up and go to a fine restaurant it's called supper, but yes," she said, a smile in her voice. "You promised me great tricks with chicken. Come on in and have some iced tea. You're probably getting eaten up by mosquitoes out there."

As if conjured by her voice, a place on his neck began to itch. He slapped at it, cursing quietly at himself, at the UnSub, at whatever strange power Holly held over him that made the thought of making love with her unendurably attractive and scared him more than the worst foe he'd ever faced.

If Eric was right—and Jack hadn't seen him wrong yet—then the stalker was watching their every move, and escalating fast.

What the hell was Jack supposed to do now? Seduce his wife to catch her stalker?

Chapter Seven

After a strained dinner, during which Aunt Bode mumbled incoherently and hardly ate anything and Uncle Virgil seemed distracted, Holly and Jack had washed the dishes.

"We're all done cleaning up the kitchen," Holly said, kissing her great-uncle's cheek. "We're going to go. We didn't get much sleep last night." Realizing what she'd said, she rushed to explain. "I mean, getting in late from the airport and getting Jack settled."

She rubbed her temple. The migraine medicine she'd taken was making it hard to think, and everything she said seemed colored by the memory of Jack's arms encircling her and his kisses tantalizing the sensitive skin of her neck.

"You'll call the Home Health Agency tomorrow?"

She nodded wearily. "I'll check with them first thing in the morning."

"Thanks for cooking supper, Jack. That was good chicken. Even Bode ate a few bites."

"Good night, Aunt Bode." As Holly kissed her aunt's forehead, out of the corner of her eye she saw Jack hand a small paper envelope to her uncle. They spoke in low tones that she couldn't hear.

In the car, Holly asked Jack about their exchange. "What were you giving Uncle Virgil?"

Jack shifted in his seat. "Tire scrapings off the curb. He can have them run through the crime lab in Jackson, see what make of tire they came from."

"Do you think my family is in danger?"

Jack shook his head. "He's interested in you. The only reason he would target your family is if he saw them as a barrier, keeping him from you. But they're not the barrier. I am."

"If he wants me, why doesn't he just come and get me?" Holly's head was starting to pound again.

"That's part of his obsession. He wants you to come to him. He thinks once he removes all the barriers, you will."

"I hate this."

Jack didn't say anything. She hadn't expected him to. He wasn't the type to offer false comfort. Paradoxically, that made her feel better and worse at the same time. He respected her, didn't discount her intelligence. But once in a while it might be nice to be held and told that everything was going to be all right, even if they both knew the words were a lie.

Back home, Holly watched Jack change from attentive husband to focused professional. The transformation sent a chill down her spine and ratcheted up the pain in her head.

"I'm sorry, but I have to lie down," she said. "I don't mean to be rude—"

Jack held up a hand. "Don't worry about it. This has been a long day. I can fend for myself. I need to unpack anyhow."

"Oh." Holly remembered something she'd thought about earlier, then forgotten. Her wedding dress and veil were hanging in the guest room closet. "You won't be able to get anything into the closet. Let me move something." She went into the guest room.

Behind her, Jack said, "It looks like a big closet. There should be plenty of room."

"You obviously didn't look inside, because my wedding dress takes up—" Her words died on her lips.

The closet was empty. The beautiful dress she'd worn for her wedding to Brad was gone. Her head throbbed and her thoughts spun dizzily. She swayed, and the edge of her vision went black.

Next thing she knew she was cradled against a rock-hard chest and supported by arms that felt like they could hold up the whole world. For an instant, she leaned into his strength, but then she straightened.

"My dress. My veil. They're gone. They've hung in this closet for six years—" She stopped on a little sob. Her hand covered her mouth.

"When is the last time you know for sure they were here?"

"I don't know." In her mind's eye she pictured a shadowy figure holding her dress, touching it. "Oh God, he took them."

Jack cursed silently and richly as he held Holly. The stalker had taken her wedding dress, just as Eric had predicted. Had the man been in the house tonight? Jack hadn't seen any signs of entry.

He'd been too damn tired to unpack last night, so he didn't know if her dress had been in the closet yesterday or not.

"Holly." He put his hand on the back of her head, caressing her soft hair for a moment before pushing her away enough to look into her eyes. He gripped her shoulders, shaking her lightly to keep her focused. "Think. When did you last open this closet?"

She wiped her eyes. "I...don't know."

"Yes, you do. Think. What else do you keep in here?"

She met his gaze, and he saw her remember. Her cheeks regained some color and her brown-gold eyes flashed.

"My suitcase. I got my suitcase out of this closet before I left for Chicago."

"And you saw the dress?"

She laughed, a short sound with just an edge of hysteria. "You can't— couldn't miss it. The skirt took up over half the closet space."

So the killer had taken it some time in the past two weeks. Maybe the day she left. Maybe tonight.

Jack led her back to the living room and urged her to sit down on the couch. He sat on the coffee table in front of her. She looked wan and tired, like the photograph tucked between the pages of Danny's case-book in his pocket.

He'd never wanted to see her looking that way again. It was the promise he always made to himself when he started a case, to do all he could to take away the victim's fear. But this time, it was more than a matter of professional pride. It hurt him deep inside to see Holly so scared and sad.

She sat, huddled in on herself, her arms crossed. "What am I going to do? I can't just sit and wait for him to do something else."

Jack leaned forward and squeezed her knees reassuringly. "You don't have to. You're not alone. I'm here," he said, knowing his words were small comfort. The UnSub was escalating *because* Jack was here.

"Now, why don't you go on to bed. I'm going to go over the closet for evidence and check in with my boss." He also wanted to arrange for some surveillance equipment. If the guy was dumb enough to come back, Jack wanted to catch him on videotape.

"No." Holly scooted away from him. "I wouldn't be able to sleep." She stood up and paced the room. "What about a video camera? Can we put in some kind of surveillance thing?" She turned to him as he stood. "I want to catch him. Now."

Good. She was fighting back. Jack smiled, admiring at her determination.

"We could put it in a cabinet in the kitchen, or in the bookcase here in the living room. Hide it, like they do those nanny cameras designed for watching baby-sitters. Are you smirking at me?" she said.

"No, I'm not. It's a good idea."

"Really?"

He nodded and she smiled. It was a shaky smile, but it sent a feeling through him that was as frightening as it was pleasant. She trusted him. It was what he wanted, what he had to have in order to protect her. He felt honored, and weighted down with the responsibility of living up to her trust.

"Now, let me get some work done. I need to see if our intruder left anything behind. You go on to bed and I'll be in soon."

She brought her gaze up to meet his, and he winced at the arc of erotic fire that flashed between them.

Bed. That place where they lay as intimately as lovers and as far apart as he could keep them. He saw in her eyes that the image in her brain was the same as in his, the two of them in her bed, covers tangled around them, drenched in passion.

He broke eye contact and struggled to stay focused. He had to think of Holly as a victim, not a woman who tempted him beyond all reason. "Go on." His voice was husky.

She stood there for a few more seconds, but he didn't meet her gaze.

Finally she ducked her head. "Good night."

She walked down the hall and into her bedroom, closing the door firmly, leaving Jack with the hollow comfort of knowing he had successfully remained detached.

Tuesday, June 24

"Yet the day wears, And door succeeds door;
       I try the fresh fortune—
Range the wide house from the wing to the center.
   Still the same chance! she goes out as I enter.
   Spend my whole day in the quest,—who cares?
But 'tis twilight, you see,—with such suites to
       explore,
Such closets to search, such alcoves to importune!"

I love it, your house, and all the things in it, because it is yours. But fast it's being spoiled by that defiler who forces you to bend to his will. Still, soon you will be with me in our secret virginal hideaway. You will be delighted that I have hung your wedding dress, that symbol of our love, in the place of honor. Do not make me wait too long, my dearest love.

THE NEXT DAY, Jack bought two mini video recorders and an assortment of hand and electric tools. He spent most of the afternoon setting the cameras up to surreptitiously record all comings and goings through the front and back doors of Holly's house.

Holly came into the kitchen just as Jack was closing the cabinet door. He wore a close-fitting white T-shirt that hugged every lean muscle, and even closer fitting jeans.

"Do you see it?" he asked.

She squinted. "No."

"Look under the door handle."

She stepped closer. There was a hole where the bottom screw should have been. "That's very clever," she said. "But that hole is tiny."

"It's big enough. The other one is in the bookshelf in the living room, just like you suggested. We'll turn them on whenever we're not here."

"Turn them on now. It's almost seven o'clock and I have my elderly aerobic class."

Jack looked up from sweeping up sawdust. She felt his gaze burn her from her cross-trainer-clad feet past her black Lycra exercise pants and bare tummy to her white sports bra. She quickly pulled on a T-shirt.

"I'll be ready in a minute," he said. "I just need to change out of these dusty jeans."

She sniffed impatiently. "I'm late."

He straightened and leveled his cool gaze at her. "I'll hurry."

A few minutes later Jack had changed into slickly pressed khaki pants and a crisp white shirt.

Holly's bones ached with exhaustion. She'd lain awake until Jack had come to bed, then she'd been acutely aware of him lying next to her, his presence taunting her, drawing her. She ached for the intimacy that she knew he wouldn't give her.

He wanted her, she knew that. But he would never let anything as unnecessary as sex interfere with his purpose. She could see in his eyes that he considered his attraction to her a nuisance and a hindrance. It was gratifying to know he was so dedicated to protecting her, but it didn't make her aching desire any easier to bear.

She wished, if he wasn't going to act on his attraction, that he'd exercise better control, because sometimes his icy gaze grew smoky and soft, his body grew hard, and she knew he was thinking about touching her. And inevitably, she responded. It never lasted, though. In the blink of an eye, his cold detachment returned and she was left exposed.

"Here we are," she said as they approached the university campus. "Turn here and you can park right across the street from the gym."

She glanced at him as he opened the car door, considering what his presence was going to do to her elderly aerobics class. He was big, intimidating, and decidedly masculine.

"Are you sure you want to subject yourself to this? There are seventeen ladies in there, all over sixty-five, who will descend upon you like little old bees on honey."

Jack closed the driver's door and came around the car, fingering his collar as he glanced toward the gym. "I go where you go. Just don't leave me alone with them."

Holly laughed. "Don't worry. I'll protect you. You know, you could join the class if you wanted to. It would help loosen up that shoulder."

Jack's lip curled. "I think not. Aerobics is not my thing. If I'd brought workout clothes, I could check out the weight machines...."

Holly swung open the heavy gym doors. "You can do that. The weight room is over to the right, on the other side of the gymnastics arena. The university supplies gym shorts and shirts. They're in the linen closet. You'll see the showers."

"Nice gym," he commented.

"The university finally put in a new floor and added the gymnastics arena. We're so proud of it. The aerobics classes are held over there on the mats."

She gestured toward them and saw the ladies coming toward them. "Here they come," she whispered.

Jack looked up to see seventeen various shades of gray atop seventeen shades of pastel bobbing toward him. He shot a quick look at the door, considering escape. He was not equipped to handle pretending to be in love with a woman who was known and adored by an entire town. *You can tell.* Eric's words echoed in his ears.

What had made him think he could do this?

After enduring effusive introductions and shaking seventeen hands ranging from skeletal and fragile to plump and pink, Jack was finally freed. Holly urged the ladies over to the mats to start warming up.

Jack fidgeted under their curious gazes until Holly got the plastic stair-steps distributed and began to demonstrate some new warm-up exercises. As she reached high above her head, her nipples stood out clearly under the stretchy sports bra. Her waist and abdomen were taut and delicately muscled and the black tight pants just showed a hint of a beautiful navel above a perfect V, right where he shouldn't be looking.

Jack glanced around the gym, because he couldn't keep looking at Holly, not while she moved like that. Not while she was dressed like that.

He quickly cataloged the exits, the various rooms, the places where someone could hide. Satisfied that everything seemed safe, he locked the exterior doors and went to check out the weight room.

After changing into shorts, he ran through some warm-up exercises, then worked out on the machines. He added several pounds to the bar at the bench press and positioned himself to do a few presses. It was gratifying that his shoulder was regaining strength. He'd be able to add more weight after a few days.

Then he ran a mile or so on the treadmill, ending up hot and sweaty and feeling better than he had in days. Glancing at his watch, he realized it had been forty-five minutes. Holly was probably about finished with her class. He jumped into the shower.

He came out of the shower room with a towel wrapped around his loins and using another one to dry his hair, just as Holly pushed open the locker room door. Her face and arms and abdomen glowed with a fine sheen of sweat, and she had a towel around her neck.

She stopped, her eyes wide as she took in his state of undress. "Oh! I didn't realize you were—"

"Sorry," he muttered, and instinctively threw his towel over his right shoulder, hiding the surgical scars, then wondered why he'd done it. He just didn't think he could endure Holly's kind concern, the look he knew he'd see in her golden-brown eyes, as if she would wipe the scars and the pain away with a touch if she could.

"No, no." She gulped. "That's okay." Her gaze

slid down, tickling his skin like the droplets of water on his chest, and lit on the towel that felt so precariously knotted.

"I'll just—" He took a step forward, gesturing toward the bench where his clothes were neatly folded.

"No! I mean— I'll leave. Um, I was going to tell you all the ladies are gone except for Mrs. Winger. Bob is always late." She licked her lips and turned away. "I'll wait outside with her."

"Yeah. Good."

Jack sighed with relief that Holly was gone, because if she'd stayed another few seconds, the damp towel knotted at his waist wouldn't have been sufficient to hide his reaction to her presence. Standing there, practically naked while her eyes laid down heat wherever they touched his wet, hot body, was more than he could take. And it didn't help that the glow her exercise had given her made her even more desirable.

Eric's words mocked him. *He'll know.*

Jack wondered if desperate, unbridled lust would do. If so, then all he had to do was keep his hands off Holly and his eyes on her.

But no, Eric's point was that the stalker would sense the difference in *her*.

Gritting his teeth, Jack forced his body back under his control and got dressed. He *would* find a way to make this work.

As he finished buttoning his shirt and smoothed back his hair, he heard a man's voice. Tucking his weapon into his holster, he shrugged into his jacket and entered the main part of the gym, prepared to meet Bob again.

Jack assessed the man who'd had the police called on him three times for domestic disputes. He was short, plump and pasty-looking, probably in his early forties. He didn't wear a wedding ring, and he stood just behind his diminutive mother.

"Jack." Holly smiled at him as he approached. "Remember Bob Winger from the post office today?"

"Hi again," Jack said, advancing on him with his hand outstretched.

Bob stared at Jack's hand for a second, then shook it.

"Do you work out, Bob?" Jack asked, allowing a shade of aggressiveness to creep into his voice. He didn't like Winger. The man was hiding something under that Milquetoast facade.

"I, uh, don't get much chance—"

"He teaches English, among his many other duties," Mrs. Winger said. "Tell him, Bobby."

Bob's face turned a blotchy pink. His shirt clung damply to his skin. "Holly already told you I teach English and American literature. And I'm the faculty sponsor for the debate team and the poetry club."

"Enough of that now, Bobby," Mrs. Winger said, irritation obvious in her tone. "I'm tired and I'm sure Holly and Jack have better things to do than listen to your tiresome list of duties at the high school." Mrs. Winger leaned forward to kiss Holly's cheek. "Thank you so much dear. I apologize for my son being late."

"Don't worry about it for a minute. I'll see you next week."

"Come on, Bobby. We still have to stop at the grocery store."

Bob followed meekly, but Jack caught the shadow of anger that crossed his round face. Was there a violent temper beneath Bob's bland exterior?

At the gym door, Bob looked back at Holly with a smile. "Holly, I'll call you."

Then his eyes briefly swept Jack from toe to head. "Nice to meet you, um…"

"Jack."

"Right. Jack." He dropped his gaze. "You know when you married our Holly you got—"

"The prize," Jack drawled. "Yeah. I know."

As soon as mother and son were gone, Jack turned to Holly. "You're mama's boy has quite a grip. He's stronger than he looks. And he hates his mother."

"I know. Did you see the look on his face just now?" She paused for a second. "He told me he really needed to talk. He asked if he could call me soon."

She started gathering up towels and throwing them into a laundry bin.

"You told him you're married now and you won't be having any more lunches and talks, I hope."

"Well, no. I didn't want to hurt his feelings. I did tell him I was pretty busy right now." She stacked up the blue plastic stair-steps the ladies had used, then picked up the little hand weights lying around.

Jack started to help her, but he got caught up in her efficiency of motion and the strength in her deceptively slim body. Besides, she was almost done.

"Don't you have a maintenance man to do that?"

"Sure. Stanley Hanks handles the gym. But each instructor is responsible for putting their own equipment away. Stanley's usually around, though. He likes my ladies."

Jack looked at how the Lycra costume molded her trim, sexy body. "Yeah, you said that before. Where is he tonight?"

"I don't know. He might be busy in the field house.

The coaches have him doing a lot of work on the baseball field.''

When she picked up her gym bag, he asked her, ''You're not going to change clothes?''

She shook her head, a shadow flickering in her eyes. ''It's kind of creepy, showering alone in here. I mean, Stanley is usually around to lock up, but I just prefer to wait until I get home.''

Jack heard the false lightness in her voice. What a jerk he was. Of course she wouldn't shower alone in the gym. That was how her husband had died.

''Am I too sweaty for you?'' she asked, her voice still a few notes higher than usual. Jack was learning that tone. It was the one she used when she was avoiding a painful subject.

Following behind her, he couldn't stop his gaze from sliding down over her supple, perfectly toned back to her firm butt moving beneath black Lycra as she walked. His mouth turned to cotton.

''No,'' he croaked, unable to banish an image of a single, salty drop of sweat trickling slowly down the hollow of her back.

Outside, it had started raining, one of those uncomfortable summer showers that appeared out of nowhere and left the air more heavy and hot than before. Holly gripped her bag and picked up her pace, hurrying toward the car.

Jack's arm slipped around her waist as the shower turned into a steady downpour. She welcomed the warmth of his hand and his sturdy support. Keeping her safe might be nothing more than a job to him, but she was becoming all too used to it.

About halfway across the double-lane highway, the staccato beat of the rain was undercut by a dull roar.

Jack's hand tightened on her waist and he urged her in front of him as the roar in her ears grew louder and closer. She looked toward the sound.

Beyond the silver-shot curtain of rain a dark shape hurtled right at them.

Chapter Eight

Before Holly could react, the full weight of Jack's body slammed into her from behind, sending her flying forward to land hard against the side of her car. His long body knocked the breath from her lungs.

Her feet lost traction on the wet pavement. She slipped. The only thing holding her upright was the weight of his body molding hers, pressing her into the warm, slick metal of her car. As she struggled to breathe, a vehicle passed close enough that she felt its heat.

Jack grunted and almost crushed her beneath his weight. Had the car hit him?

"Jack?" she croaked, unable to draw enough breath to actually speak.

Then his hands were on her and he swung her around toward the front of her car and away from the street in the wake of the dark shape. As soon as she was safely between the parked cars, he whirled back, drawing his gun with smooth swift grace.

He stood braced, aiming at the retreating car, then with a muffled curse slipped his gun back into his holster. He rushed to her and gripped her shoulders.

"Are you all right?"

She couldn't answer. All her attention was riveted on the dark street.

"Holly?" He shook her and grabbed her jaw. "Holly!"

She blinked and gasped for breath through lungs that still spasmed from the force of his body striking hers.

"Are you hurt?" His fingers tightened painfully on her arms, his face twisted in concern.

She shook her head, unable to pull her eyes away from the street where the curtain of rain had swallowed up the vision. She knew that car. She put her palms against his chest.

"Jack, that was—" she struggled for breath "—Miss Emma Thompson's car."

"What?" Jack pushed her hair out of her face. The steady brush of his fingers against her cheeks and forehead made her realize she was trembling. He pulled her close.

"Get into the car." He shouted over the drone of the rain.

Inside the shelter of the car, Holly wiped her face and tried to control her shaking limbs.

Jack quickly assessed her. "Are you sure you're not hurt?"

She shook her head. "Are you?"

He dismissed her question. "What did you say out there?" he asked as he started the engine and cool air began to blow.

Holly shivered. "I said that was Miss Emma Thompson's car."

His hand froze on the windshield wiper control. "How do you know?"

"Miss Emma's had that fifty-nine Chevy forever.

It's the only one I've ever seen. The taillights look like cat's eyes.'' She rubbed her chilled arms.

Jack cursed and pulled out his cell phone. ''What's your uncle's home phone number?''

Holly's teeth were chattering. She closed the passenger-side vent. ''Uncle Virgil will be asleep. Call T-Bone.''

Jack raised one brow. She told him the number.

''Virgil? It's O'Hara. What happened to Emma Thompson's car yesterday?''

Holly heard her uncle's voice through the cell phone.

''Okay. No. No problem. Holly's fine. I just saw a car I thought might be Miss Thompson's. Thanks.'' He put the phone back in his pocket. ''Hanes Auto Repair?''

Holly gave directions. As Jack pulled out into the street the rain stopped.

''Why didn't you tell Uncle Virgil what happened?''

''I didn't see the need at this point to give him information that might put him in possible danger.''
Danger. They'd almost been run down. They could have been killed because someone thought Jack was her husband.

''Here's the shop,'' Jack said, rousing Holly out of her thoughts.

''Yes. And there's her car.'' She pointed. ''Right where it should be, in the parking lot. But I know that was the car that nearly ran us down. See the shape of the taillights?''

Jack pulled up behind the car and got out. His jacket and pants were soaked, and clung to him like a second skin, outlining his broad shoulders and sleekly planed muscles. His hair was slicked back, emphasizing the perfection of his profile. Holly shivered not from chill, but from fear. Fear for Jack's life. He could have been killed.

For the first time, she faced that possibility head-on. In the short time she'd known him, he'd epitomized strength and safety to her, and she needed that more than she had realized. Now the idea that his life was truly in danger lodged a knot of terror in her chest so big it felt like she'd swallowed a rock. He had promised her he'd get the killer, and she'd believed him. But now he seemed human, vulnerable.

Oh God, she didn't think she could stand it if Jack died, too.

She needed to be close to him, so she got out of the car and followed him. As she came up beside him, squeezing water from her hair, he scowled at her but didn't say anything. He just went back to his calculated scrutiny of the area, his gaze missing nothing.

Holly knew by his body language when he was satisfied that they were alone. She was coming to recognize that infinitesimal relaxing of his stance, the way he shrugged, releasing pent-up tension that would not even be evident to a casual observer.

"This is the only car in the lot." He walked over and lay his hand on the hood of the ancient Chevy. "Still warm."

Holly's pulse sped up. "So it *has* been driven. But who—"

Jack held up his hand for silence. She stopped.

He took out a tiny, high-powered flashlight and shone it in the driver's window.

"Keys are still in the ignition."

"Of course," Holly said. "Mr. Hanes always leaves the keys. Someone might need their car."

Jack stared at her as if she'd gone nuts. "Are you kidding?" He cut off the flashlight, frustration hardening his voice. "Don't say it. I know. Small town. No one in Maze would dream of stealing a car."

Sudden light blinded them as several spotlights on the corners of the repair shop building snapped on. Jack reached for Holly with one hand and his weapon with the other.

Holly lay her hand on his arm. "Jack, put the gun away. I'll take care of this." She stepped away from Jack's protective embrace, hoping Mr. Hanes would be too sleepy or too incurious to wonder why she and her new husband were soaking wet in the middle of the night and snooping around.

"Hi, Mr. Hanes," she called. "It's Holly. I heard Miss Emma took out another telephone pole."

"That you, Holly? What in tarnation are you doing running around so late, and who's that with you?"

"This is Jack, my husband."

Jack lifted his hand in a self-conscious wave. Holly was relieved to see he'd left his gun in his holster.

"It's the oddest thing, Mr. Hanes," she said, walking casually toward the repair shop owner's house. "Either there's another fifty-nine Chevy in town or someone was driving Miss Emma's car over by the university a little while ago." She gestured vaguely back toward the car.

"'S 'at so?"

"Yes, sir. Did you hear anything?"

Mr. Hanes yawned and shook his head. "I watched the ten o'clock news, then went to bed. Far's I know, nobody's been messing 'round here tonight except you two.''

"Okay, then. Sorry. Jack's been looking for a classic Chevy, and he was wondering if there could possibly be two in Maze.''

Hanes harrumphed. "You best get on home, Holly. Some folks gotta work early.''

Holly smiled. "Okay. Good night, Mr. Hanes. Sorry to bother you so late.''

The lights went out and the owner of the body shop disappeared back inside his house.

Holly let out her breath in a long whoosh as she returned to Jack's side. "So, now what? Do we check the car for evidence?''

"We get out of here before the whole town comes out to see what all the excitement's about. I'll get your uncle to go over the car tomorrow. With any luck we can get a fingerprint, or a shoe print.''

"Well, anything they find will be from whoever drove it tonight, because Miss Emma keeps her car spotless.''

When they climbed back into her car, Jack grunted quietly.

Holly peered at him suspiciously. "Are you sure you're all right?'' she asked. "That car came so close! I was afraid it had hit you.''

It had. Jack gritted his teeth against the burning sensation on the right side of his back where the car's flared fender had scraped him. He navigated the rain-wet streets, his mind on their close call. Automatically, his brain calculated the timeline. They had spent about twenty minutes in the gym after Winger and his mother left. Was that time enough for Bob to get his overbearing mother home and return with Miss Emma's car?

"Tell me about the mama's boy. Where does he live?"

"Bob?" Holly frowned, obviously uncomfortable with his question.

But then, he'd already noticed that she was the type of person who chose to see the good in everyone. It was an admirable quality, but a dangerous one. Not everyone was good. In fact it was probably one of the qualities that had attracted her stalker.

"He lives with his mother, over off of Pecan Circle."

"Where is that in relation to the repair shop?"

"It's the next street over. Would he have had time? You heard Mrs. Winger. They were going to stop at the grocery store."

"I heard."

"This is maddening." She rubbed her forehead. "I don't know if I can stand wondering what this maniac is going to do next. He's trying to kill you!"

And he'd come pretty damn close tonight. Jack shifted in the driver's seat, ignoring the familiar sticky feeling of blood under his shirt. "I'm fine. He won't try anything else tonight, and with any luck, tomorrow I'll hear from the lab that they've isolated some epithelial cells from the book or one of the notes. Then we'll have your stalker's DNA. Meanwhile, the best thing we can do is stay calm and stay together."

"Why do you have to sneak around and put yourself in danger while *he* gets to roam free? Why can't you just have a citywide dragnet or something and be done with it?"

"There's nothing I'd love better than to swab every

person in town for a DNA match, but the Constitution requires probable cause to invade someone's privacy. Besides, it would alert the stalker, scare him off. And that's precisely what we don't want to have happen.''

His tone was harsh. He wasn't unaffected by the near miss they'd just had. The stalker had nearly run them both down. He was escalating more rapidly than Jack or Eric had realized.

Holly was in immediate danger. The thought made his blood run cold.

Holly muttered something under her breath as he pulled into her driveway.

''What did you say?''

She jumped out of the car and slammed the door. ''I said scaring him off sounds like a good idea to me right now. I'm ready to stand out here and scream at him to come on and get me, if that's what he wants. I can't stand this. We have no idea who he is or what he's going to do next. All we know is he wants to kill you—'' Her voice broke.

Acutely conscious that the killer could be watching them right now, Jack rounded the car in three long strides and put his arm around her, steeling himself against the supple warmth of her bare shoulder and the press of her erect nipples barely covered by wet cotton against his chest.

''Hush,'' he hissed in her ear.

''I don't want to—''

Jack clamped his fingers around her nape and covered her mouth with his, swallowing up the rest of her words. Her lips tasted salty. Ferociously driving the taste and feel of her out of his mind, he used the kiss to stop her from giving away the secret of their sham marriage.

But each time he kissed her, he found it harder to maintain his distance. His feelings were getting all mixed up in Holly's strawberry scent, the warm passion of her lips, the way she responded when he touched her.

How was he supposed to keep her safe when she was driving him crazy with need?

He tried to think about his mother, about his oath to devote his life to saving other women from such a fate. But Holly uttered a small moan against his mouth and slid her arms around his neck.

"Holly," he whispered as she kissed him back, parting her lips and allowing her tongue to touch his.

She moaned again, and this time the sound penetrated his desire-soaked brain.

What the hell was he doing? He pulled away, breathing hard. Holly's lips were swollen, her eyes dewy with desire.

Suppressing a groan, still holding her close, Jack put his mouth against her cheek. "Please, Holly. Never, ever forget that he's watching us." Her skin felt like wet shimmering silk against his lips, taunting him with the impossibility of his situation. His body ached with longing as his brain ran through the litany of reasons why he couldn't let his emotions get involved. *Her safety—her life—depended on his ability to remain detached.*

"Okay?" He put his forehead against hers as an image of his mother's limp, bruised body seared his brain. He would not let Holly become another murder statistic.

"Okay," she snapped, then added more softly, "okay."

He felt her tense body relax just a bit. He loosened

his hold, but kept his arm lightly across her shoulders. "Let's go inside, sweetheart."

She glanced at him, and in the darkness he saw her eyes glittering damply. Frightened eyes. Trusting eyes.

"Sh-h-h." He guided her into the house and gestured for her to stay still while he quickly checked the rooms. No sign that anyone had been there.

He returned to the living room, where she stood straight as a small drenched soldier.

"I don't know how long I can do this."

He stepped over to her and handed her a towel he'd retrieved from the bathroom. "As long as it takes. You have to accept that everything has changed. This sick— This person has taken over your life."

She blotted her face with the towel and tried to step around him. "Oh, trust me, I do know that. The trouble is, you've taken over my life, too."

And you've taken over mine. But Jack had to be twice as careful. He was walking a tightrope as thin as a spider's silk and as high as the Empire State Building, and he had no net. Not only did he have to convince the killer he was in love with Holly, he had to keep himself from becoming emotionally tangled up in her life.

It was a problem he'd never had before. Why was it so easy, in unguarded moments, to believe that he and Holly could really be married? When had he become so interested in family, in home, in community? Things he'd never even considered before suddenly seemed important. Like sitting across from her in the kitchen late at night and talking. Falling asleep listening to her soft breathing. Cooking dinner with her at her great-uncle's house.

He was just going to have to work harder at keeping

his mind on his job and off his vic. He caught her arm. ''It won't be much longer. We'll get him, I promise.''

She made a small, distressed sound. ''Can you really promise that? I mean, look what happened tonight. You could have been killed. Danny was a cop and it didn't keep him from being murdered.''

Jack had an overwhelming urge to promise her the moon and the stars and the Milky Way if it would take the sadness from her golden-brown eyes. He'd seen that haunted look too many times, in too many victims.

But his rational side knew hollow romantic promises wouldn't keep her safe.

He forced a laugh. ''Trust me, Holly, I don't want to die. I'm doing everything possible to make sure nobody else dies because of your stalker. We're not in this alone. There's an entire division of the FBI working on figuring out who the killer is. And what happened tonight is what we want, what we need. The whole point of my being here is to draw him out. He's getting desperate, and desperate men make mistakes.''

Her gaze held a look that Jack wasn't willing to analyze. Her eyes welled with tears and her lower lip trembled until she bit it. She blinked and a single tear escaped down her cheek. ''So we just wait? I can't go through this again. I keep thinking if I'd realized what was going on, Danny might still be alive.''

Regret and sadness slammed into him, as it did every time he thought of his friend. He knew what she meant. He felt the same way. But he knew that neither he nor she was responsible. An obsessed killer was.

He relaxed his grip on her arm and ran his fingers along the delicate curve of her biceps. ''You're not to blame for anything that's happened. That's one of the hardest things for a stalking victim to accept. It's not your fault. And we're not just waiting, Holly. Every move he makes brings us closer to him. Every mistake he makes gives us more of an advantage. I need you to be tough, to do whatever it takes to psyche yourself. You have to be convincing as a woman madly in love with her husband.''

Holly's eyes widened and that thread of awareness that was stretched to the breaking point between them zinged like a guitar string. His words hung in the air. *Madly in love.*

It took a huge effort to remove his fingers from the fascinating, soft firmness of her arm. He used the act of peeling off his soaked jacket to avoid looking at her.

Whatever it takes. He was giving her advice he wasn't willing to take himself. Because he knew what would work. If they made love, then both of them would be convincing. He hadn't needed Eric to remind him that a man and a woman who are intimate act differently around each other.

He closed his eyes. The one thing that would cinch their cover story was the one thing he couldn't do. He was an FBI agent and Holly was the victim of a crime. He'd sworn to protect her. He would not take advantage of her fear and vulnerability.

HOLLY WAS RELIEVED that Jack had stepped away from her. She couldn't stand the way he touched her, sometimes in impatience, sometimes with an achingly sweet tenderness that made her want to believe he was everything he seemed to be—including attracted to her.

''Well, that's simple enough. Be tough and act like

we're blissfully happy while we wait for him to try to kill you again, is that it?''

"Basically, yes.'' He held the jacket in one hand. His shirt was plastered to his skin and his lightweight khaki pants were so wet they were translucent.

Holly could see his boxers, and more, outlined under the wet material.

Averting her eyes, she bit her lip. "Give me your coat. I'll hang it up in the laundry room. You need to get out of the rest of those wet clothes.''

His dark gaze swept her length as his words echoed in her ears. *Whatever it takes.* She shivered and imagined herself suggesting to him that if they made love they'd be more convincing. Even as ripples of anticipation and desire spread through her like wavelets from a drop of rain in a pond, she knew she couldn't say that.

For an instant his eyes flared with a dark flame, then he dropped his gaze and started unbuttoning his shirt. She stared at the efficient movements of his fingers as he pushed each button through its buttonhole.

He shrugged out of his shirt and tossed it to her. When he did, she got a glimpse of a pink splotch on the back of his T-shirt.

Blood! Her suddenly nerveless fingers dropped the shirt. "Jack, you're bleeding.''

Jack reached over his shoulder and tugged at the wet cotton. "It's nothing. The car got a little close.''

Her heart lodged in her throat. "A little close? It *hit* you! I knew it! Oh God, why didn't you tell me? We need to call Dr. Franklin. No, we'd better go to the emergency room at Forrest General.''

He shook his head, his damp hair spiked from running his fingers through it. "I said it's nothing. I'll just take a shower."

Holly touched his shoulder blade where the stained T-shirt stuck. His muscles jerked.

"It is not nothing. Let me see it."

He pulled away. "I said no."

"Look, Agent Macho, either you let me look at that or I'm calling Dr. Franklin."

He glared at her with those glacial eyes. "What are you going to say? 'My husband got a scratch'? Don't bother. He'll just tell you to do what I'm going to do anyway. Clean and bandage it."

Holly lifted her chin and cocked her head slightly, her heart in her throat at the site of Jack's blood. "That is not a scratch. Now, you listen to me. Dr. Franklin delivered my mother and he delivered me. If I ask him to come over here to take a look at my husband's back, he will." She saw defeat glimmer in Jack's eyes and knew what he was thinking.

Small towns.

"Now take off that T-shirt."

Jack made a noise like a growl, but he turned his back and stripped off the wet shirt.

Raw abrasions furrowed along his ribs. The bleeding had stopped, but the scratches ran a good five inches across his back—he was going to be sore. She could already see the beginnings of a dark bruise.

"Your shirt wasn't torn."

"See. It's not even scratch. It's more like a strawberry burn. The car just barely skimmed me as it passed."

"Skim—" She couldn't even finish the word. She took a shaky breath. "He could have killed you."

For an instant, she was back there, protected by

Jack's body pressing her against her car, as Miss Emma Thompson's Chevy sped past. Now she knew what had happened when Jack grunted and his body jerked. The car had scraped his back.

This was life and death. This stranger who had come into her life without her permission to be her bodyguard, who took up way too much of her space and stirred desires she had suppressed for far too long, was risking his life every day to protect hers.

Tears filled her eyes as she put her hand on his shoulder. His muscles flinched. "Jack…"

Jack turned around. "I told you it's just a—"

She uttered a little cry at the sight of his bare torso. Scars crisscrossed his right upper chest and shoulder, pink against his golden skin, newly healed, like so many she'd seen in her work as a physical therapist. Her trained eye recognized them as surgical scars, the newest no more than a couple of months old.

Life and death.

"Oh, Jack."

He muttered a curse.

"You told me you'd had surgery, but this…" Holly's throat ached, her eyes were blurry. She stepped closer to him, feeling the sudden tightening of his muscles, the guarded stance. He wanted to withdraw. She laid her hand on his chest, her fingers brushing the scars. "Two surgeries? Three?"

He winced as if her touch burned him.

"What kind of man are you that you can do this, over and over again? Court death to protect a stranger?" She felt tears spill over and drip down her cheek.

He grabbed her wrist, and she waited for him to push her away but he didn't. He just stood there, his gaze dark and filled with the hunger she'd come to expect and crave.

"I'm just a man," he said hoarsely.

"No," she whispered, reaching up with her other hand to touch his cheek. "Not just a man. A hero."

His hand tightened, then pushed hers away. "Holly, don't—"

She wrapped her fingers around his nape, burying them in his thick, silky black hair, and pulled his head down until their lips were only millimeters apart. "Kiss me, Jack. Not because someone is watching. Because you want to. Because you almost died, and I need to know you're real and alive."

She felt disembodied, as if she were watching herself from the corner of the room. Was this brazen creature her? She'd never initiated anything with a man, not even a kiss. She'd always been too shy, too afraid of being rejected.

And never more than now. She had no idea what Jack would do. He'd set the tone of their relationship from the beginning. Professional, caring but stopping short of being emotionally involved. Every time they'd stepped into the privacy of her home, she'd felt it. The pulling back, the distance. He was her bodyguard, nothing more.

Her thoughts fed her insecurity and she stopped, thinking to escape with at least a smidgen of dignity before he rejected her, but he gripped her shoulders. Too late. She steeled herself for a lecture on their respective roles.

To her amazement the ice she'd expected to see in his eyes had melted into a dark flowing river and he pulled her close. She put her hands on his chest where smooth, hot skin sprinkled with soft hair overlay muscles wrapped like steel bands across his torso.

He looked at her mouth, and her insides turned to liquid heat. She'd never wanted any man the way she wanted him. He was everything she admired, everything she desired. Strength, control, determination. She reached up and touched his lips with hers, sighing softly as he angled his head.

Then he kissed her. No man had ever done the things Jack did to her with his lips and tongue. She moaned as he took her mouth in a sensual imitation of the act of love—teasing, thrusting, withdrawing, then delving again.

Holly met his erotic kiss and gave it back to him, more uninhibited than she'd ever thought she could be. She molded herself against him, losing herself in the scent and taste and feel of him, savoring his strength surrounding her.

He caressed her back, pressing her closer, until she felt the heat and hardness of his arousal against her. Her heart pounded and every molecule in her body throbbed in tandem with that steel-hard shaft that rubbed so intimately against her. She slid one hand down to touch it through his wet khaki pants, to feel for herself that it was real, that it was for her.

When she did, he gasped and tore his mouth from hers.

"Don't," he groaned, his jaw bulging with tension.

For an instant Holly ignored him. She was aching with need, blinded by desire. Then Jack grabbed her wrist.

"Stop it."

Holly twisted out of his grasp, embarrassed. "I'm sorry—" she started, but he shook his head.

When she looked up at him, his face was set, his eyes heavy-lidded, but beginning to take on their glacial edge.

"I can't..." he said, his voice choked.

Holly strained away from him, but he held her too tightly, too close. She could still feel him hot and hard against her. If they had gone much further, had he touched her the way she'd touched him, he would have known how much she was affected by him.

"Listen to me, Holly. I don't want this."

She cringed at his bald statement. Pulling away, she ducked her head. How foolish she'd been to think that finally, she had found someone she could trust to keep her safe. Someone strong and dependable. Someone who cared about her.

"I'm sorry," she whispered. "I shouldn't have—"

"Holly, you need to understand—"

Lifting her chin, she met his gaze, hers hazy with humiliation and tears. "I do understand. You're here to catch a killer. I stepped over the line. This..." She waved her hand, and a tiny sob escaped her lips. "This was a demonstration played out as silhouettes in the window for the viewing pleasure of the sick maniac out there."

She swiped tears from her face with an angry gesture. "Well, good job, Agent— excuse me, *Special* Agent O'Hara."

Jack didn't move. His shoulders were straight, his head held high, his expression blank.

She searched his face. She knew what his silence meant. This time he didn't have any comfort, any explanation for her. He'd said they needed to act like newlyweds, and acting was all he'd been doing.

A pain deeper than anything she'd ever felt, even

when her husband died, stabbed her, almost doubling her over. She tore her gaze away from his face. Feeling worse than naked in her wet clothes, she stepped away.

"I'm going to take a shower and go to bed," she said, proud of her ability to control the quiver in her voice.

He let her go without a word.

Chapter Nine

Wednesday, June 25

"God,—Who laughs in heaven perhaps, that
such as I
Should make ado for such as she—
'Defiled' I wrote? 'defiled' I thought her?"
It is not your fault, is it, my dearest love? He is
the defiler. You the defiled. You must even suffer
his lewd kisses and caresses in public. It sickens
me to see him putting his hands on you.

I saw the plea in your brown eyes as you
looked at me in the rearview mirror last night as
I sped away. You're ready aren't you? To come
home at last to me. We were so happy. We had
such fun, long ago, before others turned your
heart away. Remember your promise to me?

"Escape me? Never— Beloved!
While I am I, and you are you,
So long as the world contains us both,"
I'm so tired of waiting, my dearest love. It's al-
most time.

IT WAS HOT AND MUGGY even in the shade at the road-side barbecue place where Jack and his boss Mitchell Decker had arranged to meet. Jack hadn't wanted to leave Holly alone after their close call last night, so he'd wrested a promise from her that she would spend the morning with her aunt Bode and Debi.

He got up from the rough-hewn picnic table and paced, angling upwind from the meat smoker behind the building that belched out hickory smoke and sizzling fat. When he'd first arrived about twenty minutes ago, he'd entered the screened seating area at Wayne's Real Tennessee Pit BBQ and asked for a bottle of water, but all the young woman offered him was iced tea or cola.

He'd opted for iced tea. The ice was only a memory now.

He contemplated another glass of the sickly sweet stuff but decided his stomach couldn't take it. He wished he could take off his jacket and feel the faint breeze, but the weight of his service weapon pressing his shirt damply against his back was a constant reminder of his role, so he just kept pacing.

Holly had been subdued this morning. He'd tried to get her to take a run with him and had even offered her one of his special mushroom-and-ham omelettes, but nothing worked.

He knew he'd hurt her. But what she didn't understand and what he couldn't tell her was that he hadn't spoken last night because he couldn't. If he'd looked at her, if he'd said one word to her, he might have given in to his urges. And if he'd done that, the consequences would be far worse.

If he hoped to keep her safe, he had to keep his

mind on his job—and it was taking all his strength to do that.

She could have been injured last night, and all because he'd been distracted by how sexy her bottom looked in her exercise gear rather than paying attention to their surroundings. That car never should have gotten so close.

How was Holly so thoroughly destroying the detachment he'd built his career—his life on? The thirteen-year-old boy who had lain injured and helpless while his mother was murdered had sworn that nothing like that would ever happen again as long as he was able to prevent it.

He'd kept that oath. His life was devoted to catching killers, to saving lives. But he went home alone. He'd always thought it was better that way.

Maybe he'd always been wrong.

"O'Hara? Did I miss the turn for Hell?"

Jack looked up to see his boss walking toward him. He stood and held out his hand.

Mitchell Decker was a tall, solidly built man in his late thirties. His medium-brown hair was cut short and touched with gray at the temples. His face, with its high, defined cheekbones and straight, no-nonsense mouth, revealed nothing of what he was thinking. His direct blue gaze was intimidating to all but the most honest and straightforward of people.

When he grasped Jack's hand, Jack felt not only Decker's strength, but his integrity, his convictions and his friendship.

Decker's manner was gruff, his words few, but he watched over the Division of Unsolved Mysteries like a father over his kids.

"This isn't Hell," Jack said. "Folks from here vacation in Hell to cool off."

A corner of Decker's mouth quirked up, and he sat down. "What's wrong, Ice Man?"

Jack met Decker's gaze. "Wrong?"

"You look tired. Your new bride keeping you busy?"

Jack shot Decker a quelling glance, and quickly filled him in on their near miss the night before.

"I'll get the local field agents to help go over the car. They won't miss a molecule."

Jack nodded. "So, what's up?"

"I just came from Jackson. Divers located Ralph Peyton's car earlier. It was in the Barnett Reservoir."

"Was there a body?"

Decker nodded. "Still strapped in. Definitely male. The divers reported that the driver's seat belt had been tampered with and the door locks were jammed. And the passenger window was down."

"Are you saying someone else went into the lake with him?"

"It looks that way. They're pulling the car out now and CSI is on the scene. The body will be autopsied. I'll let you know as soon as we have the results and confirmation of the victim's identity."

"Damn." It had to be the pharmacist. Jack thought about Holly, still clinging to the forlorn hope that maybe Ralph Peyton hadn't died. His gut clenched at the thought of bringing her this news. "This is going to be rough on Holly."

"How's your bride holding up?"

Jack grimaced at Decker's use of the word *bride*. But he couldn't help smiling. "She's scared, but she's tough. And gutsy."

Decker raised his eyebrows and shot an odd look at Jack.

"What?" Jack asked, meeting his gaze.

"Nothing."

"What about Sheffield? Have they located him yet?"

Decker shook his head. "He wasn't at his last known address."

"Did the landlord say how long he'd been gone?"

"Apparently only about a week."

So one of his suspects was missing. "I'll have Virgil tell his officers to keep an eye out for him here. I assume they're checking telephone records and credit cards?"

"They are, and the chief of police assured me you'll be called as soon as they have anything."

Decker stood. "Anything else you need?"

"What about the DNA on the book and the notes?"

"The lab's got it. I'll check as soon as I get back."

"Thanks, Decker. As soon as we locate Sheffield, I want to require him to submit a DNA sample."

"Have you got anything linking him to the crimes?"

Jack looked Decker in the eye. "Not yet, but if he's the killer it's only a matter of time."

HOLLY PACED BACK AND FORTH in the sterile white corridor outside of the Cardiac Care Unit, ripping a paper cup into shreds, and being no less hard on herself. She was a medical professional. How had she allowed this to happen?

"Hol, come and sit down. You're wearing a hole in the floor, and you're making a mess." Debi bent down and scooped up shreds of paper cup off the floor.

"Aunt Bode is in good hands. The doctor said she was doing okay."

Holly squeezed her burning eyes shut and allowed Debi to brush the remaining bits of shredded paper out of her hands. She rubbed her temple. "The doctor said 'as well as can be expected.' That's not the same as okay."

Debi pulled her into the waiting room, where a television was dialed to CNN and a large group of people were apparently using their relative's heart attack as an excuse for a boisterous family reunion.

"I should have seen it coming," Holly said, as Debi urged her toward a chair on the other side of the room from the loud extended family. She perched on its edge, unable to relax enough to sit back. "She was coughing. Her face was pale. I should have been paying more attention."

"You are so hard on yourself. Aunt Bode's been coughing for years. Please relax. You want some more water?"

"What time is it? Jack should be back by now." Holly gave a little hiccuping laugh. "I can't even call him. I don't know what his cell phone number is. He probably didn't want me to have it—"

"There he is," Debi interrupted, touching Holly's arm.

Holly twisted in her chair. There he was. He stood there, tall and rock steady, his gaze cataloging the room. Holly's burning eyes and pounding temples felt soothed just by the sight of him.

Before she even realized she was moving, she was out of the chair and across the room and flinging herself into his arms. "Jack!" She burrowed her nose in the hollow of his neck and breathed deeply. The scent of soap and sun filled her senses. "I am so glad you're here."

His arms tightened around her. "Your uncle's neighbor told me about your aunt."

She nodded as he cradled her head in his hand. She loved it when he did that. His strong sheltering hand made her feel like nothing could hurt her. A shiver wracked her and she clutched at his shirt.

"Hey," he whispered. "It's okay. I'm here now." He covered her hand with his and gently unclenched her fingers. "Let's go sit with Debi."

As he led her by the hand back to her seat, all eyes in the waiting room were on them. She pulled away and sat down. "I'm sorry," she whispered to Jack. "I shouldn't have made a scene."

He reached for her hand again and kissed her knuckles, sending a wave of grateful warmth through her.

"You didn't make a scene. Now, tell me what happened. How's she doing?"

To Holly's relief, Debi gave Jack a rundown of Aunt Bode's collapse, the 911 call, and the twenty-minute drive to Forrest General Hospital in Hattiesburg. "Holly rode in the ambulance and I followed in the car. We called Uncle Virgil, and he came straight from the police station."

"He had to drive by himself. I should have—"

Debi shushed her. "You did everything right, Holly. Why are you so hard on yourself? She did great, Jack. She had me call while she performed CPR. She probably saved Aunt Bode's life." Debi patted Holly's hand. "Now sit back in that chair and relax. I'm going to get you some water."

Holly watched her sister pour a cup of water. She shook her head. "She's been wonderful," she told

Jack. "It's like something in her snapped when Aunt Bode collapsed. She just stepped right in and took over. She's doing the things I should be doing. I should be taking care of *her*."

"I think Debi takes after her big sister a lot more than her sister realizes."

There was a note in his voice that Holly hadn't heard before. A sort of affectionate amusement. She glanced up at him and found his dark gaze on her, two faint frown lines between his brows.

"Did you talk to your boss? Is everything okay?"

He nodded. "Sure. I'm just worried about you."

"There's something wrong. I can tell. What did you find out?"

"We'll talk about it later. You look tired. What do the doctors say about your aunt?"

"She had a massive myocardial infarction. A heart attack. She's on a ventilator."

Debi handed Holly the water. "They say she's doing as well as can be expected," Debi added. "It's Uncle Virgil I'm worried about. He's with her now."

At that moment, Virgil appeared in the doorway. Debi immediately went to him and led him over to where they were sitting.

Holly and Jack got up. Jack put his hand on Virgil's arm and Holly hugged him.

"They say she's stable for now," Virgil said, his voice unsteady and wavery, like an old man's. "She looks so small in that big bed."

Holly's eyes stung with tears. He and her great-aunt were all the parents she and Debi had known for most of their lives. She'd never thought of Uncle Virgil as old, but he was two years older than Aunt Bode. And right now he lookcd frail and stooped, and the lines in his face looked deeper, as if he'd aged twenty years in the past two hours.

"Uncle Virgil, why don't you let Debi take you home. I'll stay here tonight."

Virgil McCray straightened and shook his head. "Nope. I never spent a night away from my Bode and I ain't about to start now. The nurse told me I could sleep here in one of these recliners. She said they have blankets and pillows."

"Then, I'll stay with you," Holly said, sending Jack a warning glance when he opened his mouth.

But the immediate rejection of her statement came from Debi. Holly frowned at her sister, who had crossed her arms and was looking down her nose at her.

"*I'll* stay with Uncle Virgil. We'll sleep side by side there." She indicated two empty recliners. "Jack, my sister looks terrible. Take her home. She needs a good night's sleep."

If Holly hadn't been so worried about her aunt, she'd have turned pink at Debi's unspoken warning to Jack to let Holly sleep undisturbed tonight.

Jack put his arm around her, and it was all Holly could do to keep from collapsing against him. "I think you're right. We'll be back over here early in the morning. Call if there's any change." He squeezed Holly's shoulders. "Come on, Holly. I have orders to put you to bed."

"I don't think—"

He leaned over and kissed her quickly on the mouth. "You don't get to think. You're outnumbered."

HOLLY LAY IN BED listening to Jack's movements through the house. He had the same ritual every night, and every night she lay awake until he climbed into bed beside her. He didn't know that, of course. She always pretended to be asleep when he came into the room after making sure all the doors and windows were secure.

Tonight would be different. She doubted she'd be able to sleep at all, even with Jack's disturbing yet comforting presence beside her. Her mind and heart were still back at the hospital with Uncle Virgil and Debi. She'd hated to leave them alone, but as Jack had said, she was outnumbered. Even Uncle Virgil had joined in, saying he and Debi would be just fine.

She mentally checked off the list of things she needed to take to the hospital tomorrow. She'd stop by her aunt's house and pack a bag with her robe, slippers and toiletries, and Uncle Virgil's shaving kit. If she had time, she'd make Uncle Virgil's favorite cinnamon muffins. He'd be up roaming for breakfast at the crack of dawn, complaining about the hospital food.

The door opened quietly and Jack slipped into the room. He had on a white T-shirt and boxer shorts, and in the faint light that sneaked in around the edge of the blinds, his lanky, long-muscled body was the most beautiful thing she had ever seen.

She watched him quietly and expectantly, anticipating his movements as he completed his nightly ritual. He walked around the bed to the double windows. She heard him lift the edge of the blinds and knew he was peering outside, as he did every night. Then he looked at her.

Her back was to him, but she didn't have to see him to know his gaze was on her. What did he think each night when he stood there, watching her in the faint light? That another day had passed and he still hadn't identified her stalker? That soon this would all be over and he could go back to his life?

Or did he think what she thought? That he would give anything if the bed they shared wasn't divided by the insurmountable barrier that existed between them. The barrier of a madman who would not rest until Jack was dead.

He came around the bed and slipped between the covers, barely making a sound. He lay on his back with his arm behind his head and stared at the ceiling.

"Jack?"

"I wondered if you were asleep. Are you okay?"

His familiar question made her heart flutter. He'd asked her that many times in the few days they'd known each other. It was comforting—one of those little habits that developed between two people who loved each other.

If only.

Her mouth softened into a smile, but it faded as her thoughts returned to her only remaining loved ones. "I can't stop thinking about Aunt Bode." Fear swirled in her belly like nausea. "She may be dying."

He took his arm from behind his head and turned toward her, leaning up on one elbow. "Holly, I know you're scared. But you're a health professional. You know this could be a long ordeal while your aunt recovers. You can't be there every minute. You've loved her and cared for her all these years. She knows that. Whatever happens, you will have done all you can. I haven't known you very long, but I know that much." The harsh line of his jaw softened.

"What you need right now is rest. That's what's going to do your family the most good. Then tomorrow you can relieve Debi and stay with Virgil.'' His voice was gentle.

As usual, he didn't offer her false assurances or empty promises. Her eyes filled with tears. She'd heard the most important thing he'd said. *Whatever happens.* She knew he was right. She just didn't want to accept it.

The awful hollow fear that had lurked inside her most of her life started to grow. ''Uncle Virgil and Aunt Bode took us in after our parents died. I owe them so much. They're the only family Debi and I have.''

''Sounds like a nice family.''

The wistful regret in his voice stung her heart. He had come here as her bodyguard to protect her. He had taken her on as his responsibility, and his presence made the unbearable more bearable.

If she could do anything for him, she would lift the regret and sadness he carried like a shield. He was so honorable, so dedicated to protecting others, but he wore his professionalism like armor around his heart. Holly wanted to know why. From his awkward words just now, she was terribly afraid she already knew.

''Jack, who was the person you cared about who was killed by a stalker?''

He stiffened, and tension radiated from him like a fever.

''It was someone in your family, wasn't it?'' The tightly leashed grief in his voice when he'd told her that first night had made that obvious.

''That subject's not open for discussion.'' He punched his pillow and stretched out, as if preparing to relax for sleep.

Holly wasn't going to accept that. "You brought it up before."

His jaw muscle twitched. "I was making a point."

She almost reached out to him, but he seemed so remote, so cut off from her right then. "Do you make that point to all your assignments?" She intended her question to provoke a response, but it came out sounding more bitter than sarcastic.

Their forced marriage and the intimacy that had grown between them was blurring the boundaries between what was for show and what was real. Sometimes when Jack kissed her she couldn't tell the difference. Her feelings toward him were changing, and she realized that she wanted to be more than just a victim he'd been assigned to protect.

He wiped a hand over his face, then pushed his fingers through his hair. "It was my mother," he admitted, his voice so hushed that she almost didn't hear him.

"Your mother? Oh, Jack." It was what she'd expected, and yet so much worse. Tears stung her eyes. Her heart felt ripped to shreds by razor-sharp claws. She touched his arm, feeling his muscles flinch under her fingers.

"How old were you?"

She leaned over closer and put her hand on the side of his face, forcing him to look at her. He met her gaze reluctantly, his eyes as bottomless as black holes in the dim light.

He took a deep breath and turned his face away, resisting her touch. "I was thirteen. My stepfather wouldn't leave her alone. We'd moved, even changed our telephone number. But he found us."

His voice was emotionless, but Holly heard the terror and hurt behind his flat tone. "He was in a rage that night. If he couldn't have her, nobody could. He broke down the door. Knocked me across the room. Then he strangled her."

Only thirteen, and he'd witnessed something so horrific that she couldn't even imagine it. How had he stood it? In her mind's eye she saw a skinny, black-haired boy lying injured on the floor, watching with fiery eyes as a man he knew, probably a man he'd once thought he could trust, choked the life out of his mother.

As if he'd read her mind, the blackness in his eyes turned to ice. "I testified against him. I put the psycho away—" Despite the bravado in his words, his voice broke.

With his words, Holy realized something very important about Jack O'Hara. He wasn't cold and aloof because he didn't get emotionally involved. It was a defense mechanism, part of his shield. What he did was not just a job. It was his own personal crusade to keep what happened to his mother from happening to others.

Jack resisted the impulse to throw himself up and out of bed, away from Holly's soft golden-brown gaze, from her comforting touch, from her quiet compassion.

Nothing in his life had been as devastating as watching his mother die. Nothing he'd done since had felt better than standing in that courtroom and hearing the verdict against his stepfather. If he were truthful, he'd have to admit that each time he started on an assignment, each time he caught a killer, he was searching for that same satisfaction, that knowledge that he'd stopped another one. But nothing had ever made up for the despair of knowing that he couldn't save his mother.

Until Holly had come into his life.

Now he was beginning to understand that there were things more important than a lonely crusade. Suddenly he found himself wondering how it would feel to just let go. Let himself care for Holly.

Helpless terror streaked through him. He couldn't afford that luxury. If he let himself be swayed by emotion, he courted failure. And if he failed, she would die. He pushed the pillow behind his head and rubbed his eyes. He had to quit thinking of Holly as a woman. He couldn't afford to forget for a minute why he was here.

''Jack, don't.''

He frowned and caught her wrist before she touched his face. He couldn't bear her touch right now. ''Don't what?''

''Don't throw that icy barrier up. Not this time. I need you.''

The catch in her voice cut a deep furrow through his heart.

''I need to be held, I need to be reassured that I'm not alone, at least for tonight.''

Jack lay frozen in place, his chest tight, his heart throbbing painfully. He released his breath in a long sigh, knowing he shouldn't be shocked. He'd seen it coming. Ever since last night when she'd risked rejection by touching him so intimately. Her desire and her courage had awed him.

God help him, he wanted her, too. But if he gave in to his desires, he'd be proving to himself that he wasn't the best man for this job.

''Okay,'' she said in a small voice. ''I'm sorry. I

shouldn't put you in this position. I suppose all your assignments fall a little bit in love with you.''

A little bit in love. The words hit with the force of bullets, tearing through his flesh, embedding themselves in his heart. He'd heard the words before. Many exhausted, frightened victims had turned to him, mistaking relief and gratitude for something more. It was one of the reasons he found it doubly important to set the tone of the relationship from the first moment, and why he never got involved.

But there had been something special about Holly from the beginning. He'd known the first moment his eyes met hers that she was different. And sure enough, she'd turned his life upside down.

She hadn't given over control of her life to him, depending on him to make her safe. Just the opposite. She'd resisted, clinging with all her might to every bit of control she had.

A little bit in love. Was she? He looked at her, hating the thrill of hope that sent his heart racing. He cursed himself for wanting to believe that her feelings were more than just the natural and temporary attraction between the victim of a stalker and her bodyguard.

Despite his best judgment, he leaned up on one elbow and rubbed his fingers across her knuckles where she gripped the pillow.

''I'm supposed to be protecting you.''

Holly nodded. ''You are. Since you've been here I've felt safe for the first time in a long, long time. But I'm worried and afraid. I need someone to hold onto tonight. Can you truly say you don't want me?''

Jack groaned silently as his body reacted to her plea. ''It's not that simple. I've wanted you from the first moment I saw you,'' he whispered. ''What I don't want is this." As if to illustrate his statement, he moved closer, allowing her to feel how forcefully she affected him.

She gasped as he pressed his arousal against her.

He was in bed with the only woman he'd ever met who could destroy the detachment he'd spent twenty years perfecting, and it was taking every ounce of strength he possessed not to cross the remaining few millimeters of snowy cotton and wrap her in his arms.

Her eyes were wide and glittery in the dim light. Hurt welled like tears in their amber-brown depths. "I don't understand."

"Neither do I." He reached up and pushed a strand of hair off her cheek. "I just know I don't have the strength to resist you any longer." His body tightened painfully, his arousal grew heavy and even harder, his heart quickened. "I've never done this before."

She began to tremble. "Done what?"

It was the middle of the night. He was in bed with his wife. And he had suffered through two long, painful nights of unslaked desire. To his dismay, his hand shook against her cheek.

"Made love to my wife," he whispered raggedly, awed by the words. He'd never dreamed he'd ever say them. He'd never even considered marriage. Letting people close was not something Jack O'Hara did easily.

But Holly was changing him. Her bravery, her honesty, her genuine caring were melting through his self-imposed barriers like a blowtorch through ice.

He pulled her to him.

She came eagerly, a small whimper escaping her lips as his arms encircled her. Her skin was heated, her body supple and yielding as he flattened his palm on the small of her back so that every inch of her body pressed against his.

As his mouth sought hers, his hand slid downward. He pushed her cotton nightshirt out of the way and cupped her bottom, that firm, rounded bottom that drove him crazy each time he looked at it.

He bent over her, kissing her deeply, torturing himself by holding back. He felt like a teenager, his body throbbing with a need so great he thought he'd lose control any second.

As he settled on top of her, she accepted him, shy but yielding when he urged her legs apart with his. He looked down at her, his senses filled with the image he'd built in his mind of this moment. The reality was so much more beautiful. Her hair was a dark velvet scarf draped over the white pillow, her eyes glinted with amber fire in the darkness, and her mouth drew him like a sailor to a siren's song.

He sat back, pulling her with him, and slid her nightshirt off over her head. His breath caught at his first sight of her bare breasts. As he cupped their perfect roundness in his hands and bent his head to taste them, Holly cried out and arched her back, lacing her fingers around his neck.

He lifted her to gain better access to those taut, rosy nipples. Then he touched and tasted all the places he'd fantasized about for three days.

Her body fascinated him. She was strong, firm, yet decidedly feminine. The silk of her skin over her long, smooth muscles acted like an aphrodisiac, sending him toward the point of no return. Her stomach muscles contracted as he ran his palm over them.

He loved everything about her. Everything. Her stubborn need to stay in control, her compact, supple strength and her responsible nature destroyed all his preconceived notions about women.

Jack bent and ran his tongue down her ribs to her perfect navel, tasting the sweetness of her skin. His mouth watered as he anticipated moving farther, down her belly, to taste what would certainly be the sweetest nectar of all.

She gasped and her fingers fisted in his hair.

"Jack." Her voice was breathless and panicky.

He froze, his heart pounding, his breathing raspy in the quiet room. If she said no, he could stop. He could.

He closed his eyes. He hoped he could.

"I'm scared."

He lay his head on her gently rounded belly, feeling her unsteady breathing. "Me, too."

She might be talking about the killer who had targeted her, but Jack wasn't. Holly might never understand how afraid he was. He'd never felt this way before. Right now he felt more naked and exposed than he'd allowed himself to feel since the night his mother died. It was terrifying, and yet strangely seductive.

Holly was strong, capable, able to take care of herself. That made her sexy as hell to him.

He sat up and peeled off his clothes, then lay beside her again.

Holly trembled with desire. The feelings he'd coaxed from her with his hands and his mouth had been too much to bear. The urgency and force of her own response had surprised and frightened her.

She didn't remember ever feeling as turned on as she'd been with Jack's hands and mouth roaming over her. She'd never thought of herself as a sexual person until that instant before she'd stopped him, terrified of losing herself in uninhibited response to the sensations he was evoking in her.

He'd said he was scared, too. Was he? She traced his face with her fingers, searching for the truth. His eyes never wavered as she touched his cheek, his nose, the corner of his mouth.

Her heart in her throat, she let her fingers drift down his jawline, his neck, the strong curve of his shoulder. He gasped as she lightly touched the dark, flat aureole of a nipple, feeling it harden under her fingertip.

Something changed in his face, and he grabbed her wrist, startling her.

No, she begged silently. *Don't stop me this time.* She didn't think she could ever work up the courage again.

He kissed her fingers. ''Holly,'' he said, pushing her hand down his muscled stomach. ''Touch me.''

A thrill of desire melted her insides to liquid fire. She could hardly breathe as she trailed her fingers down, down, with his hand guiding, until she felt him, hard and straining, against her palm.

He groaned quietly and moved his hips slowly, rhythmically, as she shyly stroked him. Then, in a swift, smooth movement, he lifted himself above her and touched her as intimately as—more intimately than—she was touching him. An instant of embarrassment washed over her as his fingers slid easily inside her. She knew she was slick and ready. Her body revealed what she couldn't say. She needed him desperately.

He drew a swift breath as he stroked her once, twice, three times, bringing her closer and closer to the brink. ''Jack.''

He slid into her, hot, hard, filling her. At the same

time he kissed her. She was engulfed in him, surrounded by his lean strength, and she felt more frightened and yet safer than she'd ever felt in her life.

She met him, stroke for stroke, kiss for kiss, until sensation surrounded her and everything faded to black except the two of them.

Chapter Ten

Thursday, June 26

> "He is with her; and they know that I know
> Where they are, what they do: they believe my
> tears flow
> While they laugh, laugh at me."
> Oh my dearest love, why do you hurt me so?
> "Will you cast For a word, quite off at last
> Me, your own, your You?"
> Of course not. Not you. Still, time grows short
> and I grow impatient. Do not betray me, my dear-
> est love. Oh, no, not you. And then I think…
> "Is one day more so long to wait?"

HOLLY WOKE the next morning with her head on
Jack's shoulder and his arm cradling her. She woke
easily, quietly, moving into wakefulness with a sense
of safety and comfort she couldn't remember feeling
since she was a small child. Had it been that long since
she'd felt safe and cared for?

She knew it had.

Her thoughts lingered for a moment on the night,
and the incredible magic of Jack's lovemaking. But the

haze of bliss faded as she came fully awake. She needed to call the hospital and check on her great-aunt.

She carefully slipped out of Jack's embrace.

"What time is it?" he whispered, his fingers gliding sensuously down her naked back as she pulled away.

She looked at the clock on her bedside table as she rummaged around in the covers for her nightshirt. "Six-twenty. I intended to be up before now. Go back to sleep. I'll wake you in a little while."

He opened one gray eye and peered at her. "Are you okay?"

The question thrilled her. She'd been so afraid he would revert to the official Jack this morning. "Just worried about Aunt Bode. I want to get to the hospital early." She couldn't stop herself from smiling at him. She pulled on the nightshirt. "But I'm fine."

"Good," he murmured, his eyes drifting shut.

Holly watched him for a minute, her eyes feasting on his broad shoulders, the lean sculpted chest and abs, the side of one hip revealed by the casually draped covers. His face, relaxed in sleep, looked young and vulnerable, not harsh, in the early morning light.

Reluctantly leaving the room, she headed for the kitchen to start the coffee and call the hospital. Then she'd bake a pan of Uncle Virgil's favorite muffins.

When she flipped on the kitchen light, her gaze fell on Jack's wrinkled jacket, the one that had gotten soaked the other night. She had tossed it onto the washing machine, thinking she'd hang it up later, then had forgotten about it.

She picked it up and reached for a coat hanger. The jacket seemed heavier on one side. Feeling the pockets, she fished out a small leather-bound notebook.

Holly stared at it for a moment, stunned. *Danny's casebook.* Jack had told her he hadn't seen it.

She opened it, recognizing Danny's familiar scrawl. Her heart ached as she read the notes that sounded so much like him. She touched the pages, missing Danny's quick laugh and caring attitude. He'd been a good friend.

She glanced in the direction of her bedroom, frowning. Uncle Virgil must have given the book to Jack, although why Jack hadn't bothered to tell her she couldn't imagine.

A wave of irritation flowed through her. Jack was arrogant, he could be really annoying when he was in his official mode, but he'd been open with her about every aspect of the case. Why then, hadn't he mentioned that he had Danny's casebook?

Hoping that Danny had written something that might trigger a memory and provide a clue to the killer's identity, she flipped through the book. Just as she remembered, Danny had faithfully chronicled each day when he was working on a case. She'd sat here in her kitchen many nights with him while he carefully recorded everything she told him about her fiancé, her husband, the notes she'd received.

Toward the last of the filled-in pages a name caught her attention.

Jack.

Her pulse pounded in her throat. Jack? She squinted at Danny's hurried scrawl.

March 7. Called Jack O'Hara at the FBI for assistance regarding possible stalking case involving Holly McCray Frasier.

Danny had gone to Jack for help? She stared at Jack's name. Was it a professional contact or had they known each other?

Holly felt a twinge of doubt. Jack hadn't mentioned that he had Danny's casebook, and he'd never given her the first indication that he'd talked to Danny about her case. What was he hiding from her? And why?

Holly pushed her fingers through her sleep-tousled hair. Her defenses were crumbling. She hadn't realized how much she'd come to depend on Jack, on his uncompromising honesty—

"Holly?"

Holly jumped at the sound of his sleepy voice. Her fingers clenched around the book.

Jack wore jeans slung low on his hips and no shirt. His eyes were still heavy-lidded with sleep, and as he absently ran his fingers across his chest, Holly's mouth went dry at the remembered silky steel of his skin.

She swallowed and pushed away the memory of their lovemaking. No, she couldn't call it lovemaking. She'd thought last night that it was, but now, knowing that Jack had deceived her about Danny, could she trust anything about him, including his motivation for taking her to bed?

She held up the book like a small shield. "Why didn't you tell me Danny contacted you about my case?"

She had the brief satisfaction of knowing she'd surprised him. His brows shot up, his eyes turned glacial, and his lanky, relaxed stance went rigid.

"Where did you get that?"

"From the pocket of your jacket. You lied to me. Uncle Virgil didn't call you, Danny did."

She turned to the page and held it out. "He wrote this on March seventh, about two months after he started investigating Ralph's disappearance. Danny asked for your assistance, and now he's dead. What took you so long, Agent Macho?''

"Look, Holly, Danny and I had been friends for a long time. He and his family were there for me when my mother was murdered. When he called I was in the middle of a case.''

"Friends? That's why you're here? Because Danny was your *friend?*''

"Holly, I came here because of Danny, but—'' Jack was interrupted by the telephone.

Holly slapped Danny's casebook closed and reached for the phone. "It's probably Debi, wondering where I am.''

"It's barely seven o'clock,'' Jack started, but she quelled him with a glance.

Jack cursed himself for forgetting that Danny's casebook was in his jacket pocket. He looked at the leather-bound book Holly clutched. He knew he should have told her about Danny, but damn it, was this case destined to strip away every last vestige of privacy he had? He'd barely talked about his friend's death to anyone, even to Decker.

All he'd wanted to do was come here and solve this case for Danny's sake, then leave. He hadn't wanted to reveal his personal grief about his friend's death, or his guilt that he hadn't responded in time to save Danny's life. He certainly hadn't wanted to get emotionally involved with the stalking victim.

The memory of last night pummeled him.

Too late now. He was involved. Nothing had ever affected him like making love with Holly. Her loving, tender touch had healed a wound inside him that had ached for a long, long time.

A change in her manner drew his attention. She'd bowed her head and her body had drawn in on itself.

"No," she whispered. "Oh, Debi, no. When?" Her breath escaped in a sob.

The shock and anguish on her features ripped at Jack's newly raw emotions. He knew what she was hearing by the naked anguish in her eyes. Her great-aunt had died. Not knowing what to do, he stepped toward her, reaching for the phone. He could at least talk to Debi, find out what happened.

But Holly backed away. Amber flame lit her tear-filled eyes, warning him not to come any closer.

"Twenty minutes ago? How's Uncle Virgil?" she said, then bit her lip as she listened to the answer. "I'll be right there, okay? You wait for me. I'll take care of everything." She set the phone down, then stared at it for a few seconds.

She took a deep breath and faced Jack, her expression serene, but sadness darkening her eyes to maple-syrup brown.

"Your aunt?" Jack asked unnecessarily.

"She died about twenty minutes ago. I should have stayed." The simple words condemned him and the things they had done in the night.

"There was nothing you could have done."

Her jaw twitched. "You obviously don't know anything about family," she accused him. "I could have *been there.*" Her lower lip trembled, but she clenched her fists and raised her chin.

She was holding onto control with a fierceness that Jack had not seen in anyone he'd ever known. He thought she might break, she was wound so tight.

"You need to let go," he whispered. "It's okay to cry."

Her breath caught in a sob, and she lifted one hand without releasing her fist at all. "I—can't—let—go." She shook her head. "If I do—" She met his gaze, hers filled with terror.

"If you do, I'll be here to catch you." He reached out to her, and this time, although she didn't yield, she didn't back away. He carefully wrapped his arms around her, hardly even touching her, just surrounding her with whatever support he could offer.

She was so stiff. So afraid. So alone. He knew how she felt.

For the first time since he could remember, Jack wished for the courage to connect with someone emotionally. He forced his memory back to the days after his mother's murder. The terrifying loneliness, the empty ache that he'd known even then would never go away. And he thought about what might have helped him. He hugged her just a little tighter.

Holly didn't bend.

"I know you're scared," he said. "I know it hurts. Let go for a minute. There's nobody here but you and me. Nobody will know. Nobody will see."

She crumpled then, and he caught her, pulling her close, cradling her head, murmuring things to her that he'd wished someone had said to him, finding that saying them to her helped him, too. The ache of loneliness inside him shifted, morphed into yearning—a yearning to share her pain and thereby lessen it. "It's okay. You can be brave and strong later. Right now just lean on me."

Holly's arms came up around his neck and she clung to him. The feel of her embrace, of her wet face pressed into the hollow of his shoulder, built in him the urge to make the world right for her.

And somehow, she'd made him actually offer a hug. What was she doing to him?

Holly wanted to sink into Jack's strong, invulnerable chest and hide there. But she couldn't. Her beloved aunt was dead. Holly had responsibilities. She needed to check on Uncle Virgil and Debi, start making arrangements for the funeral, prepare Uncle Virgil's house for the dozens of visitors who would be showing up with casseroles and sympathy.

She didn't have time to indulge in self-pity. She pushed away and wiped her eyes.

"I've got to get ready. I should already be there. I need to help Debi with arrangements." Instead she'd spent the night here, indulging herself in forbidden delights with a man who was here for only one reason, to assuage his guilt about not saving his friend.

Her anger returning, she stepped out of reach of his embrace. "Here," she said, thrusting Danny's casebook toward him. "You might need this."

She walked past him, out of the room.

Jack watched her, weighing the damning evidence of the book in his hand. He had no excuse but his own cowardice for keeping the information from her. He'd been trying so hard to stay behind his emotional shield that he'd done the unforgivable. He'd lost the trust of the person he'd sworn to protect. And that wasn't all.

His fear may have lost him the one person in the world who could teach him how to love.

His cell phone rang. It was Decker.

"Jack, the locals in Jackson are planning to pick up

Sheffield either today or tomorrow.''

''Great. Tell them to call me. I'll drive up—'' He stopped. He had no idea what was expected of him as Holly's husband. But he knew she was going to need him.

He shook his head. What was he thinking? His number one priority was catching the killer. He'd like to be there to give Holly emotional support, but what she really needed from him was to be free of this madman.

''Jack?''

''Tell them I want him brought in for questioning. I don't care what they charge him with. I'll drive up.''

Jack turned off the phone and went to get dressed. He came out of the guest room about the time Holly emerged from her room.

''You okay?'' he asked.

She shook her head. ''I don't know. I feel kind of numb. I have to go. There are arrangements to be made with the funeral home and the florist. And people will be coming by the hospital and Uncle Virgil's house. Are you going with me?'' she asked.

''Of course. I'm your husband.''

She frowned at his words, and he knew she needed a real husband to help her through this grief-laden time. But he wasn't a real husband, and before the day was over, he was probably going to have to leave her alone.

''Holly, I'll help in any way I can. But if I get a call I'll need to drive in to Jackson. They're pulling Donald Sheffield in for an interview. This may be our first good lead in your case.''

She stared at him, fear shadowing her sad eyes, and

he wished he had more to offer her. He wished he had the courage to be a real husband, to give her more than just the facts.

He wished he had the courage to give her his love.

Chapter Eleven

Friday, June 27

"Not a word She said, but, in a gentle humbled way,
  (As one who had forgot herself in grief)"
Ah, my dearest love, it hurts me so to see you grieve.
I want to reveal all, to stand beside you proudly as
your true love. I long to help you bear this grief. But
no, not yet. It would not be seemly, so close to death.
  "Yet I will but say what mere friends say,
    Or only a thought stronger;
  I will hold your hand but as long as all may,
    Or so very little longer!"
I will play the part of the helpful friend, but you will
know and I will know, that soon all pretense will be
over and we will finally live as one.

EVEN KNOWING how well respected Uncle Virgil and
Aunt Bode were in Maze, Holly was still overwhelmed
by the outpouring of sympathy and caring from their
friends and neighbors. There had been a constant
stream of visitors bringing food and offering condolences.

Jack had been by her side all day yesterday, quietly

supportive. Although Holly could tell he'd never been in this situation before, he'd helped her make all the necessary arrangements with calm efficiency, earning him a new level of respect, as well as her everlasting gratitude. She noticed that he never let down his guard, though. He observed everyone he met with his sharp eagle's gaze.

This morning, however, he'd gotten a call and had to leave to go in to Jackson. She had hoped he'd make it back in time for the viewing at the funeral home this evening, but he hadn't.

Now, two hours later, as she stood in the living room of Uncle Virgil's house, accepting hugs and comforting pats as people came and went, she found herself observing her neighbors and acquaintances like she never had before. Being around Jack had given her a new, suspicious perspective.

Jack's words echoed in her ears. *You need to observe, analyze, catalog. The person who is stalking you could be your grocery clerk, your best friend, your pastor.*

As she nodded and smiled at neighbors' comments about how natural Bode looked or how well Virgil was holding up, she observed, and tried to curb her apprehension. One of these people was a murderer.

She also kept an eye on Uncle Virgil. He was restless, wandering back and forth from one room to another, talking to friends, shaking hands, nodding and smiling his gruff, warm smile. Occasionally he would wipe away a tear or pull out his handkerchief.

Debi continued to surprise Holly. She had blossomed in the role of gracious hostess. She made sure every guest was greeted at the door and that every dish was labeled and listed for thank-you notes later.

Mrs. Ross, Holly's neighbor, sought her out. "Where's your husband, Holly?" she asked, her bird-like eyes darting here and there. Holly figured Mrs. Ross had the concept of cataloging every person down pat.

"He had to be in Jackson today. He'll be here soon."

Mrs. Ross snorted. "He should be by your side at a time like this. Not a very considerate husband, if you ask me."

"Actually, Mrs. Ross, he was by my side all day yesterday, helping me make the arrangements. And he's a wonderful husband. He's a very good cook, too." *And a better lover.* She wished she had the nerve to say that out loud to the woman. It was something her aunt Bode would have said.

Holly smiled to herself as she remembered how carefree and flamboyant her great-aunt had been. Mrs. Ross gave her an odd look and skittered away to speak to someone else.

Holly had started across the room to check on Uncle Virgil, when a hand on her arm stopped her.

"Holly."

It was Earl Isley, the insurance salesman she'd dated once.

"Earl," she said, giving him a frozen smile. "How nice of you to come." Earl was just an inch or two taller than her, and nice looking, with a spare tire at his waist. He'd moved to Maze several years ago, after his divorce. His wife and two kids lived in Hattiesburg.

Holly had never thought of him as other than a nice, boring guy. But tonight, recalling what Jack had told her about the insurance policies, she cautiously took a step back from his too-close stance.

"I'm so sorry about your aunt. Virgil came to me a few years ago when Mrs. McCray started becoming forgetful. He wanted to make sure their insurance covered home care."

Holly nodded. "I know," she said. "Thank you. Now if you'll excuse me—"

"I made a special effort to be here. I usually spend Tuesdays and Fridays with my kids." He smiled, and his eyes flickered down the front of her dress and back up.

Holly nodded, trying to be polite, but edging away from him. Then what he'd said hit her. "Tuesdays and Fridays?"

Jack considered Earl Isley a suspect, since she'd included his name on her list. He could be her stalker. He had all the attributes. He was quiet. His job certainly wasn't fraught with stress.

Maybe she could find out some information from him. "Your children live in Hattiesburg?"

"With their mother. It's not a bad drive. Take Tuesday for instance. I took them to see a silent film, *The General* with Buster Keaton. Then we had pizza. They love to eat pizza late at night, although their mother claims it keeps them from sleeping."

Holly's pulse beat in her temples. Had she just learned a vital clue? If Earl was in Hattiesburg eating pizza with his kids, he couldn't have been the driver of Miss Emma Thompson's car. Or was he trying too hard, providing an alibi when no one had asked for one?

"Thanks, Earl, for taking time away from your kids to visit. But I really must pay attention to the other guests."

Holly hurried toward Uncle Virgil, feeling Earl Isley's gaze tickling the back of her neck like a spider's web.

WHEN JACK GOT BACK to Maze after eight o'clock, he headed toward Virgil's house. Holly had told him the viewing at the funeral home would be from five until seven. Afterwards, people would gather at her Uncle's house for visitation.

The evening was overcast, the promise of rain hanging heavily in the air. Jack positioned the air conditioner vent so it blew on his face. It had been a long and frustrating day.

By the time he'd gotten to Jackson, the detectives had picked up Sheffield. Ironically, they'd hauled him in for violating his restraining order. When the police had finally tracked him down, he'd been at the apartment of the woman who'd taken the order out against him.

As soon as Jack identified himself as FBI, Sheffield had requested a lawyer. While Jack waited for the court-appointed lawyer to free up some time, he'd gone to visit the ex-girlfriend. She was a textbook partner in an abusive relationship. She swore to him that Sheffield had changed, and that she was having the restraining order removed. Sheffield had promised he'd never hit her again, as long as she stayed faithful.

Looking at the woman's swollen left cheek, colored the distinctive pale green of an old bruise, Jack cursed himself for an idiot, but still wasted several minutes explaining to her that not all men used violence and threats to win their loved one's heart. The woman nodded, but Jack knew his words fell on deaf ears.

Back at the precinct, reining in his anger and swearing if Sheffield ever lifted one hand against Holly he would tear him limb from limb without blinking, Jack interviewed the cowardly creep about his relationship with Holly. Sheffield was hostile and arrogant, calling Holly stuck-up and saying he wouldn't waste his time with her.

"Then why do your telephone records show that you called her less than two months ago?"

"I didn't call her," Sheffield lied baldly. "I got better things to do with my time."

"Like beat up your girlfriend?" Jack shot back, earning a reprimand from Sheffield's lawyer.

He spent the rest of the day with the Medical Examiner and the Crime Scene Unit of the Jackson Police Department. Jack had been informed yesterday that the body pulled from the reservoir was Ralph Peyton.

However, the autopsy of the skeletal remains was inconclusive. There was no evidence to indicate that Peyton had been shot or stabbed before his body had gone into the water. It was impossible to determine if he'd been dead or alive when the car went down.

Although the car tag and registration positively identified Ralph Peyton's car, the murky waters of the Barnett Reservoir had deposited a fine layer of silt over the entire interior and exterior surfaces, effectively destroying any possible trace evidence that might have proven the presence of a second person or given a clue as to the cause of Peyton's death.

Jack came away more frustrated than ever. He knew they'd have a hard time proving Ralph Peyton was murdered, with no physical evidence on the car. He couldn't even rule out Sheffield, because the man had refused to give an alibi for the day and time Miss Emma Thompson's Chevy had hurtled toward Jack and Holly. His lawyer told Jack that if and when charges were brought, they would discuss his client's whereabouts.

As Jack pulled up in front of Virgil's house, he looked at his watch. He was surprised at the number of cars lining the streets this late in the evening.

Jack got out of the car and shrugged self-consciously, settling his jacket onto his shoulders. He didn't belong in this world. He had no understanding of the kind of love that brought people together to support each other in their sadness.

His mother had been the only family he'd had, so after her death he'd been handed over to Children's Services and had lived in a series of foster homes until he turned eighteen.

As he approached the house, Jack observed the crowd through the front window. Far from what he expected, the men and women were talking easily, smiling, eating and drinking coffee or iced tea. Holly had called this "visitation."

Shaking his head, he rapped lightly on the door. A stranger opened it. Jack opened his mouth to explain who he was, but the man immediately held out his hand. Jack shook it.

"Earl Isley," the man said. "And unless I'm mistaken, you're Jack O'Hara."

Jack controlled his expression and smiled blandly. "That's right." He studied the man Holly had dated briefly. Isley was a decent-looking guy. He looked normal, just like most serial killers.

"So, Jack, when all this is over, why don't you give me a call?" Isley dug into the breast pocket of his jacket. "Have you considered increasing your life insurance now that you're a married man?"

Suppressing an urge to laugh at the man's persistence, Jack accepted Isley's card. "I hadn't, but maybe I should. Now if you'll excuse me, I need to find my wife."

Stepping past Isley, he swept the room with his gaze until he spotted Holly's familiar chestnut hair. Relief washed over him, so sharp and sudden it was like being doused with a bucket of ice water. He headed toward her, but was stopped by a feminine hand on his arm.

"Hey, hunky husband."

He met Debi's gaze. "Hi, sis. Did you do what I told you to?"

Debi leaned in to whisper in his ear. "Keep an eye on Holly? Sure. Every minute."

"Good." He looked back toward Holly. "How is she doing? How…are you doing? All of you?" Hell, what were you supposed to say at these things?

"We're doing okay. You sure are jumpy, though. Maybe you're hungry. Holly's over there by the dining room table."

"Yeah, I see her. Thanks."

"Jack…"

He didn't miss the odd note in her voice. Had Holly told her about their sham marriage? He steeled himself for sisterly outrage.

"How did you and Holly fall in love so fast?"

He wasn't expecting that. Her words left him speechless. He felt his face grow warm. He swiped a hand across the back of his neck.

"It is *so* not like Holly to be spontaneous, and I get the feeling it's not like you, either. But something obviously clicked between you two."

"What do you mean?"

Debi grinned. "Come on. You should see your eyes when you look at her. I saw you at the hospital, too. Both of you lit up like Christmas trees when you saw each other."

Jack's face got even warmer. His mouth dropped open but he couldn't think of a thing to say.

"Hey, don't get embarrassed. I think it's cute. Now go on, Holly's been watching the door, waiting for you to show up."

Something obviously clicked. Jack tried to dismiss Debi's comments. She'd probably always been a romantic, making up love stories to fit any occasion.

He picked his way through groups of people, occasionally stopping to verify that, yes, he was Holly's husband, or to speak to someone he'd already met.

He made a note of everyone he recognized. Uncle Virgil, of course. Bob Winger's mother was helping herself to the sandwiches and chips from the table. He glanced around, but at first he didn't see Bob.

Then he spotted him, standing alone in a corner of the living room, his eyes glued to Holly. Just the fact that Winger was looking at her raised Jack's hackles. He moved quickly toward her, blocking Winger's line of sight with his body.

Holly was talking to Stanley Hanks. When she saw Jack, her face lit up.

His heart fluttered like a kid's. Was she glad to see him? He was certainly glad to see her. She looked sedate and slender in a simple gold dress that made her eyes gleam with amber light. The sight of her soothed his burning eyes and eased the tension in his neck.

"Jack, hi." She smiled at him and slid her arm into the crook of his.

"Hi, yourself." He ran his fingers down her forearm to clasp her hand as he kissed her cheek.

"You remember Stanley Hanks?"

"Sure. How's it going?" He didn't bother to hold out his hand, he just met Hanks' gaze and nodded.

Hanks nodded and mumbled something about it being nice to see Jack.

"Stanley, thank you so much for coming by. You don't know how much it means to me. Will you excuse me now?"

"Sure, Holly," Hanks said. "I'm real sorry about your aunt."

Jack watched the other man's face, but all he did was smile briefly at Holly, then head for the food-laden table and pick up a plate.

Jack put his arm around Holly and pulled her close.

"I can't believe Stanley came," she said. "He never goes to these things."

As she leaned against him, he breathed deeply of the strawberry scent of her hair, calmed and stirred by the soft firmness of her body against him. "You okay?" he asked.

"I'm doing really well. And Uncle Virgil is doing better than I expected. I was afraid this was going to be so hard."

Jack's gaze roamed over the crowd. "Looks like everyone in town is here. Your aunt must have been well-liked."

"People are here because of Uncle Virgil. Funerals are about the living, to ease the pain of grief, and provide some closure. I think Uncle Virgil is going to be okay."

"Yeah." For Jack, a guilty verdict had gone a lot

further than an impersonal ceremony had in terms of closure. "How about you?"

"I'm going to miss Aunt Bode, but her mind died a long time ago. I'm sad, but I think she's in a better place now."

Jack squeezed her shoulders. He was relieved that she wasn't devastated by her aunt's death, for her own safety as well as her emotional health. He needed her to be focused, not prostrated by grief.

Out of the corner of his eye, he saw Winger's mother motion to him. But Bob ignored her and started toward Holly, his eyes still watching her with that unwavering stare.

"Bobby!" a voice shrieked. "Bobby! Help me!"

Jack turned in time to see Mrs. Winger drop into a dining room chair, her attention focused on her son.

At the sound of her voice, Bob stopped in his tracks. A shadow of anger passed briefly across his face before he turned his attention to his mother.

Holly started toward them, but Jack caught her arm. "Let's see what happens," he whispered.

"But she's sick."

He shook his head. "I don't think so."

"Mama, what is it?" Bob asked, frowning.

"I'm feeling faint. I think those cold cuts must have had MSG in them." Mrs. Winger fanned herself.

"Mother, you're making a scene." Bob's eyes flashed with anger and his voice rose in pitch. "Now, just have some water and sit for a minute."

"No. You have to take me home, now. I can't stay here another minute."

So Bob escorted his mother out of the house, his face red and his expression stony as people watched and whispered.

Taking their cue from Mrs. Winger, people began to say their goodbyes and leave.

"Poor Bob," Holly said.

Jack stared at her. The man could be a killer and she was feeling sorry for him.

As he shook his head in wonder, she lay her hand on his forearm. "Guess what? I think we can eliminate Earl Isley from the list."

"Eliminate? What are you talking about?" He looked around and noticed that a couple of the stragglers were watching them curiously. "Let's get out of here. We need to talk, about several things."

Holly's chin went a fraction of an inch higher. "I should stay with Uncle Virgil tonight."

Jack's neck was tight, his shoulder ached, he was frustrated by his inability to get a handle on Holly's stalker, and he really didn't feel like dealing with her stubbornness tonight.

"You are not staying here. Debi is doing a fine job of taking care of your uncle Virgil. And there's no way I'm letting you spend the night away from me."

Chapter Twelve

Holly climbed into bed and leaned back against the pillow. "So when Earl started talking to me about seeing his kids on Tuesdays and Fridays, I realized he might have an alibi. He told me he'd spent Tuesday evening with his kids watching a Buster Keaton film at a silent film festival in Hattiesburg, then he took them for pizza afterwards."

Jack shifted restlessly.

"So he couldn't have been the one in Mrs. Thompson's car."

Jack raised a brow. "And he just happened to start talking about what he was doing on Tuesday night?"

"Yes. He was just making small talk I guess. You know, there's not much to say to grieving families after you've expressed condolences."

Jack rubbed the back of his neck. "Or maybe he mentioned it to give himself an alibi. Whoever is doing this is clever. He's killed three people and hasn't been caught. You can't take what anyone says at face value. Any man in that room could be the killer."

Holly's pulse thrummed in her temple. She thought the same thing. She couldn't look at anyone now without wondering. "What about you? What did you find out today?"

Jack told her about Donald Sheffield and relayed the information that Ralph Peyton's body had been found. "Someone may have been in the car with him," Jack told her. "Someone who escaped through the open passenger window, leaving Ralph to drown, trapped by his own seat belt."

"Oh my God, poor Ralph." Holly felt the snare of danger tightening around her like a noose. She moved closer to Jack. "You know, for a few minutes while I was getting that information from Earl without making him suspicious, I felt in control of my life. I felt like maybe I was even helping to keep you safe."

Jack was silent and unmoving. It was comforting for Holly to have him so close, but the barrier was still there.

"You don't need to keep me safe, Holly. I told you, it's my job—"

"Stop saying that!" she cried. "I do. I need desperately to keep you safe. Don't you understand?"

Jack held out his arm and, despite her vow not to let him touch her again, she slipped easily and naturally into his embrace. She lay her head against his chest.

"Maybe I do understand," he said softly. "Tell me about your parents. What happened to them?"

She was mildly surprised at his change of subject. What did her parents' death have to do with anything? But his arm around her and his warm breath against her hair coaxed her into talking.

"My father was a journalist. My mother taught English at the college. She would go with him when he went out of town, and Aunt Bode and Uncle Virgil would keep Debi and me. I still remember listening to Mama telling Aunt Bode what to do if something happened to them. It was always fun staying with Aunt Bode. We'd sit up late at night and watch scary movies, and talk about Mama and Daddy going on dangerous adventures, like on television. I imagined them battling monsters.'' She paused. ''I was always so relieved when they got home.''

''And then one time they didn't come home?''

She nodded, laying her cheek against the sinewy muscles of his chest. ''And I couldn't help but believe the monsters got them, although I know it was a small-plane crash.''

''And now this monster is after you.''

She burrowed a little deeper into the warmth of his chest, wincing in expectation of the low rumble of his laughter. But tonight was a night of truths. ''Please don't laugh at me.''

Jack put his finger under her chin and lifted her face to look into her eyes. ''I promise I will never laugh at you.''

And Holly believed his promise, just like she believed everything he told her, even that he could keep her safe.

Jack's other hand caressed her bare shoulder as his finger traced the line of her jaw. His eyes were smoky and soft in the darkness. Oh God, she was afraid she was more than just a little in love with him.

He touched his lips to her forehead. ''I'm going to do my best to keep you safe. We'll get this guy.''

But then what?

She ducked her head, afraid of the feelings his lips and hands were stirring within her. She took a long breath filled with his soapy, sunny essence.

"Tell me about Danny."

He went perfectly still.

"Why didn't you tell me you knew him?"

He shrugged and straightened, and Holly felt his withdrawal like a chill breeze. Was he going to refuse to talk to her now?

He wiped a hand down his face. "At first it didn't seem relevant. I didn't think anyone needed to know how I'd come to find out about your case." He sighed. "I guess I didn't want you to think I might be swayed by personal feelings. Hell, maybe I didn't want to think it of myself."

"You were good friends?"

"The best." His voice was muffled by a suffocating regret. "He was always there for me. His parents took me in for a while after my mom was killed. Then, the one time he asked me to be there for him, I went and got myself shot and couldn't respond until it was too late."

"That's when you had the surgeries on your shoulder?" Holly's compassion swelled until her throat felt tight. "I'm sorry. Poor Danny. If he hadn't gotten involved with my case—"

"Don't even think that." Jack clutched her shoulder. "Danny was a good detective. If he had to die, at least he died the way he'd have wanted to, trying to stop a murderer."

Holly shuddered. "Jack?"

He pulled her closer and placed his cheek against her hair. "Yeah, hon?"

She splayed her palm across his taut abdomen. "Make me feel safe."

He growled deep in his throat and pulled her to him, covering her face and neck and breasts with his kisses, until everything fled her brain except the heady, erotic sensation of him making love to her.

Saturday, June 28

"So I soberly laid my last plan, to extinguish
the man.
Shall become first peace out of pain,
Then a light, then thy breast,
O thou soul of my soul! I shall clasp thee
again."

The fates are with me now. Once more shall I stir the potion. Once more shall I milk the venom. Then he will be no more and you will be free. And my dearest love, if you will not come to me even then, well be damned. I'll come for you.

THE NEXT MORNING, as they were dressing for the funeral, Decker called Jack to tell him the FBI lab had managed to recover DNA from the textbook, although they'd gotten nothing from the note. Decker told him not to get his hopes up, because they had also recovered some latex, which suggested the presence of surgical gloves. But it appeared that someone may have sneezed or coughed on the page Jack had marked.

Jack knew the likelihood was small that the DNA recovered from the book was the killer's, but maybe it was enough to get a warrant for Sheffield's DNA.

Decker had more news too. The CSI team that had gone over Miss Emma Thompson's car had found a partial footprint.

"The assay shows mud, bits of gravel and sand, and calcium carbonate and magnesium carbonate."

"Is that significant?"

"Well, from what I understand, calcium magnesium carbonate is dolomite, which is extremely rare in that part of the country, although calcium carbonate, which is limestone, is fairly common. But I suppose the gravel could have been imported. They're assaying a control sample from the parking lot now."

"Thanks, Decker. Tell them I need something unique, something I can hang a killer on."

He'd wait for the facts, like he always did, but he couldn't help but feel a sliver of satisfaction. Maybe this case was coming together, after all. He shrugged on his jacket and checked that his weapon was securely fastened into his belt holster.

"Who was that?" Holly asked as she walked into the kitchen, fiddling with an earring. She was dressed in an ankle-length black dress, dark stockings and slender black pumps. A string of pearls and pearl stud earrings were her only adornment. The black made her golden-brown eyes look huge and trusting.

Jack swallowed, reminding himself that they were going to her aunt's funeral and he shouldn't be thinking of the silken skin and firm curves under her dress.

"That was Decker, my boss. He had a couple of things for me. They did find a partial footprint in Miss Emma Thompson's car, and they recovered some DNA from the textbook."

Holly's eyes grew wider. "DNA? Will you be able to match it with Donald Sheffield?"

He nodded as they got into the car. "I've asked the Jackson police to get a warrant for his DNA. It's a cinch he won't provide it voluntarily. I want to drive up there this afternoon to be there when they execute the warrant. I don't want anything to screw this up."

He glanced over at her as he backed out of the garage. "If that's okay with you."

"That's fine." Holly fingered her pearls, staring out the car window.

"Are you okay?"

She nodded, and he saw her swallow.

"I dread this," she said.

He pulled out onto the street and headed for the funeral home. "I know."

"I've been to a lot of funerals. It's expected in a town like Maze, but this is family."

He nodded, willing himself to keep his mind on Holly and not let it drift back in time to the worst funeral he'd ever sat through.

A memory hit him unawares. The bright, hushed Baptist church where his mother's funeral had been held, thanks to the generosity of Danny's parents. They had taken him in as soon as he was released from the hospital, and had paid for his mother's funeral.

Jack remembered sitting with Danny on one side of him and Danny's mother on the other, his broken arm throbbing with pain, as the preacher made kind but impersonal statements about the murdered woman he'd never met, and the child orphaned by her death. No one else was there. No one brought casseroles or comfort to the thirteen-year-old boy who had watched helplessly as his stepfather wrapped his hands around his mother's neck and choked the life out of her.

"You had to bury your mother," she murmured.

He winced. Sometimes she was a mind reader. He didn't answer, hoping she'd move on to what she really wanted to talk about, which was her aunt's funeral today.

"How did you stand it?"

She was just looking for reassurance, he told himself. She only wanted to hear that it was possible to stand anything. "You stand it. You get through it and you go on, because that's what people do." He squeezed her hand briefly.

"You're so calm, so controlled. I wish I could be more like you. I'm—" she caught her breath in a little sobbing gasp "—I'm a wreck."

He shot her a quick glance. Her eyes were glittery with unshed tears, but her back was straight and her chin was lifted. Deep inside, Jack felt a glow of pride and admiration for her. "You're doing great. I've never known anyone like you. You spend all your energy worrying about other people, and all your time doing things for them. You're strong, physically and emotionally. When you get your mind set on something, you never give up, which may or may not be a good thing." He looked for a smile, but she was watching him somberly.

"Hey," he said, touching the corner of her mouth. "Smile for me."

She shook her head. "I don't think I can bear it if you die, too."

The words hit his heart with a thud. He wasn't planning to die. That wasn't what scared the crap out of him. The trust and hope and, yes, even love, in her small, strained voice were what just about did him in.

He pulled into the parking lot of the funeral home and turned to her. "I'm going to do my best not to die, Holly."

Jack reached out and placed his palm against her cheek. She closed her eyes and lay her hand on top of his. "And if I can help it, nobody else is going to die because of this bastard."

BY THE TIME the funeral was over, Holly felt as fragile as a teacup too close to the edge of a table. Her great-aunt had never had children of her own, and for many years it had been obvious to Holly that caring for her and her sister was a burden to Bode. But she'd been vivacious and fun-loving, and she'd taught them how to cook, how to dress and how to have fun with life. The saddest part of losing her was remembering the person she'd once been.

Uncle Virgil had done well. Debi had sat beside him and he'd held her hand the whole time. Somehow, while Holly had been doing her best to take care of her family, they had learned to depend on each other. It was a gratifying feeling, if a lonely one.

All Holly wanted to do now was go home and sleep for a day or two, preferably with Jack at her side. The outpouring of love and sympathy from the people of Maze was heartwarming, but it was also exhausting. It seemed that every single citizen of Maze had turned out for Aunt Bode's funeral.

Holly saw a new side of Jack, tall and elegant in his dark suit, as he greeted strangers and fielded questions and comments. He stood like a bulwark between her and the cloying sympathy of the well-meaning but sometimes suffocating neighbors and friends.

After a poignant graveside service during which it started to rain, Holly was ready to take Uncle Virgil home, and make sure he and Debi were okay.

As they rode back to the funeral home in the limousine, Holly put her hand on Jack's arm. He automatically covered her hand with his and bent his head.

"After we spend a little while with Uncle Virgil and Debi at his house, we should be able to go home."

Jack gave her a guilty look. "Do you think you

could ride with them? I need to be in Jackson when that DNA warrant is executed. Sheffield could be our man.'' He glanced at his watch. ''If I leave five minutes ago and drive like hell I can make it.''

As sudden and sharp as a slap in the face, the reason Jack was here hit her. He'd played his part so well, she'd forgotten.

There was a killer out there, and Jack was here to catch him.

Comforting the victim, making her fall in love with him, was just a perk of the job. Holly winced. She was overemotional right now, and unfortunately, she'd allowed herself to depend on Jack way too much in the few days he'd been here. She'd better get used to handling things alone again.

Tears she'd held at bay all day pricked her eyelids. ''Sure. I can ride with them. No problem.''

''Unless you'll go with me. I wish you would. I'd prefer not to let you out of my sight.''

And she savored every second by his side. She considered going, just to be with him. But the idea of spending hours at the police station in Jackson, not to mention the possibility of facing Donald Sheffield, was more than she could handle. She shook her head.

''It's okay. I know you don't want to leave your family right now. But promise me you won't go anywhere. The only person that's going to be investigating suspects is me. Got that?''

Holly noticed Debi straining to hear what they were saying from the opposite seat of the limo, at the same time as Jack smiled and kissed her nose. More acting.

She nodded and pasted a smile on her face. ''I understand, *dear.* But you hurry back.''

His gaze burned her, reawakening the hunger that licked at her insides like flames.

"Oh, I will."

THE RAIN HAD TURNED into a downpour, and Uncle Virgil was pale and stiff with fatigue by the time Holly got him into bed with a cup of hot soup and made him promise to take a long nap.

She kissed his leathery cheek. "Uncle Virgil, are you okay?" she whispered.

He nodded and sighed. "My poor Bode. She was pretty today, wasn't she."

"She was beautiful," Holly agreed. "Now, you drink that soup and sleep for a little while."

"I miss her already."

"I know. Me too."

"What about you and Debi?"

"We're just fine. Don't you worry." Holly turned out the lamp and stepped quietly over to the door.

"Holly?"

She turned back to look at him. At seventy-three, he was beginning to show his age. His hair was completely gray and his shoulders, which Holly always remembered as so broad, were bent and stooped. But his eyes were still sharp and his hands were still strong.

"You've been stuck here way too long. I'll be police chief of Maze as long as I can do the job. And your sister is going to be fine."

Holly nodded. "I know."

Virgil took a sip of the hot broth, then cleared his throat. "You need to leave this town."

She was shocked. "Uncle Virgil, are you telling me the town's not big enough for the both of us?" she joked.

He shook his head. "Nope. I'm telling you it's not big enough for you. You ought to go back with O'Hara to D.C. Get started on a family. Pay attention to your own needs for a change."

Holly stared at her great-uncle, worry clouding her mind. Was he becoming forgetful? "Jack is here to find the stalker. When he does, he'll go back to his job, and I'll still be right here." She deliberately kept her voice light. "Don't forget, we're not really married."

"Oh, I think you are."

Her face burned under his sharp scrutiny as her body remembered Jack's lovemaking. "You need to take a nap, Uncle Virgil. You're obviously overtired."

"Don't get smart with me, young lady. I know what I'm talking about," Virgil said, as she closed the door.

Back in the living room, Debi had fixed two glasses of iced tea. "What was Uncle Virg saying?"

Holly shook her head. "He's talking crazy. Saying Jack and I should leave town."

"He's right." Debi traced a drop of condensation down the side of her glass.

"What?" Holly almost choked on a swallow of tea. "You want to get rid of me too? What is this, some kind of conspiracy?"

"You've been acting strange for a while now, but you and your hunky husband are obviously in love. And as long as you stay here, you'll be teaching free aerobics classes, working too hard at the hospital, trying too hard to keep me on track, and spending too much time over here cooking supper for Uncle Virgil. If you don't get out of Maze, you're liable to lose your handsome hunk."

"Can't you just call him Jack?" Holly said irritably. Why suddenly, was everyone so concerned about her?

"Sure, but it's so much fun to watch you blush."

"I don't blush." Holly took another sip of tea and considered her sister. Could she tell her the truth? That Jack was here to catch a killer, and soon would be gone?

How would she explain it? She'd never thought about the aftermath. What was she going to tell the people of Maze once Jack was gone?

Oops. Marry in haste, repent at leisure.

We discovered that mutual lust wasn't enough to build a marriage on.

See, Jack is an undercover agent. He was just pretending to love me, to catch my stalker. Oh, didn't I mention that I had a stalker?

She shook her head to silence the voices.

"Holly, I want to apologize to you."

"What?" She blinked at her sister. "There's no reason—"

"No. I need to. What I said that first night when I met Jack. About the men around you dying. I'm so sorry—"

"Debi, there's something—"

The doorbell rang.

Debi groaned.

"I love this town," she said dryly. "You'd think they'd leave the grieving family alone for five minutes, wouldn't you?"

"I'll get it." Holly sighed, getting up.

Debi peered out through the sheer curtains. "It's Bob Winger's car. He probably has his mother with him. I can't take those two. I'm going to go take a shower." Debi headed toward the back bedroom.

Holly opened the door and found Bob Winger on the doorstep, holding a dish.

"Hi, Holly. Mother sent me over to bring you a cherry pie."

"How nice." Holly reached for the pie. "Will you come in?" She couldn't not invite him in, but she held her breath, hoping that he was in a hurry, or that his mother had told him to be right back to take her to the grocery store. The last thing she wanted this afternoon was to listen to Bob's problems.

"I, uh…" He looked past her. "Are you alone?"

Holly frowned. "No. Debi's in the back, and Uncle Virgil is in his room taking a nap."

"What about your husband?" Bob finally relinquished his hold on the pie. It was still warm.

She took the dish and set it on the table near the door. "He should be back any minute now," she lied. She had no idea how long Jack would be, but she wasn't going to tell Bob that. Were you looking for him?"

"No, no. I just—" He paused. "Holly, listen." Bob opened the screen door. "I've missed being able to talk to you."

Holly sighed. "Bob, I really can't today. I need to be here for Uncle Virgil. We can have lunch next week."

"We could go get a latte at Benson's Restaurant. Mrs. Benson just put in an espresso machine."

The look on Bob's round face was so needy, so hopeful, that Holly couldn't force out the words to turn him down. She made one last effort. "Why don't we stay here? I'll make coffee and we can have a piece of your mother's pie."

Bob winced. "I wanted to talk about—" He looked down. "Well, you know."

Holly did know. Bob was conflicted about his sexuality, and for some reason, he'd chosen Holly to confide in. She'd made it a point to be understanding and nonjudgmental, and so, over the past few years, Bob had come to depend on her.

But Jack had warned her to stay put.

She assessed the man she'd befriended. From Jack's point of view, he was a suspect. Did she believe Bob was a killer? She couldn't imagine it, but then, she couldn't imagine anyone she knew killing three men in cold blood.

She pushed open the screen door and stepped out onto the porch. The rain was still falling and the clouds had darkened the sky.

"I'll sit out here for a minute if you want to talk, but that's the best I can do. I really don't want to leave Uncle Virgil for long."

Holly sat in the porch swing and Bob sat in one of the wooden rocking chairs.

"I've really missed our talks since you got married so suddenly, Holly. You make life more bearable for me." He looked out at the rain. "'Because thou hast the power and own'st the grace to look through and behind this mask of me and behold my soul's true face.'"

Holly's heart leaped in her chest, cutting off her breath. Bob had never quoted poetry to her before.

"What—What was that poem?"

His face turned pink. "Oh, I'm sorry, Holly. I didn't realize I'd spoken out loud. That was Elizabeth Barrett Browning. One of my favorite poets."

Holly gasped quietly. Robert Browning's wife.

"What did you want to talk to me about?" she asked, measuring the distance between the porch swing and the door, and realizing she'd have to go past Bob. She glanced at the porch rail. Could she jump it without landing in the bushes?

"You know I've always had trouble connecting with people. I blame my father. He left my mother when I was just a baby. He treated her badly, made her succumb to him, then just discarded her. I think I've always hated him and all men because of that."

Bob had talked about his father and his hatred of men before. But today there was an odd tone in his voice. He seemed agitated, verging on hysteria.

"Bob, what are you trying to say?" She remembered Jack saying her stalker's purpose was to destroy the men who had defiled her, taken her purity. Bob's ramblings sounded ominous.

"I've never been comfortable around women, either, except for you. You are the only person who really understands me."

Alarm bells were clanging in Holly's head, so loudly that she wanted to cover her ears. She stood and walked over to the porch steps, pretending to look up at the sky. "I really need to get back to Uncle Virgil, Bob."

"No!" He jumped up from the rocker and grabbed her hand. She tugged, but Jack was right, Bob was surprisingly stronger than he looked. She stared at his thick fingers, wrapped securely and painfully around her wrist.

"You're hurting me," she said, straining against his grip, her heart slamming against her chest wall. "Let go."

"I can't. Please calm down. I don't want to hurt

you. I just need to talk.'' His eyes looked wild, sweat poured down his face and neck, his cheeks were bright red. ''Please don't struggle.''

She considered screaming, but the rain was beating a loud, continuous rhythm on the porch roof, drowning out other sounds. Screaming wouldn't help.

''Okay,'' she said soothingly. She relaxed her arm, then suddenly twisted it down toward his thumb, using a technique she'd learned while teaching her self-defense classes. Just like the book said, Bob's thumb gave way and her wrist was free.

''I'll talk to you for a minute, Bob. But don't touch me again or I'll have to ask you to leave.'' She watched him carefully, wondering if she could lure him over to the edge of the porch and push him down the steps, then get inside and bolt the door before he recovered.

''I want to get away from my mother,'' Bob was saying. ''I hate her. Sometimes I think I hate everybody. Nobody is nice to me. Nobody cares about me. I need to do something about Mother before she smothers me to death.''

''Why—why don't you move out?''

Bob laughed. It wasn't a pleasant sound. ''Move out? You don't understand. She thinks she can't live without me. She's probably right. If I moved out of her house, she'd probably die just to show me. I'm afraid I'll never be free. I wish she was dead.''

''You don't mean that—''

''Yes, I do!'' Bob shouted, his face bright crimson and his fists clenched. He shook with rage. ''I wish it every day. I can't get away from her any other way.''

Holly's heart stuck in her throat as she cautiously watched Bob's eyes. She adjusted her stance, balancing her weight so she could defend herself if he attempted to grab her again.

Maybe his outburst explained why he hadn't already made his move to possess her. He felt trapped by his mother.

What if he'd already killed the woman?

"Bob, I think it might help if you talked to a doctor. Remember, you said you'd think about it?"

"No! I need to talk to you." Bob grabbed for her arm again, but Holly blocked with her forearm, sending a crushing pain all the way through to her bones.

"What are you doing, Holly?" Bob asked, stricken. "I don't want to hurt you, but if you don't listen to me, I can't be responsible for the consequences."

"I told you, don't touch me again." Fist clenched, body balanced, Holly stared at the man she had thought was mild-mannered and quiet, trying to imagine him tripping Brad in the shower and forcefully banging his head against the concrete floor, forcing Ralph to drive his car into the lake, getting close enough to Danny to somehow kill him with wasp venom.

Her brain couldn't make the leap. Bob was meek and fearful, hiding behind his mother. Was there really another, deadly side to him?

"You need to go, Bob. If you don't, I'll call T-Bone to come and get you."

"Why are you treating me like this?"

Holly heard footsteps treading on the stairs up to the porch. A figure appeared out of the rain. Backing away from Bob, she turned and threw up her hands against a muscled chest.

"Holly!"

She looked up into the soft blue eyes of Stanley Hanks.

"Stanley," she breathed, relieved. "I thought you were Jack."

Stanley frowned. "What's the matter? What's going on?" His large, rough hands steadied her as she regained her balance.

"I'm…fine," she said, her breath coming in ragged bursts because of her pounding heart. "Now."

Stanley stared at Bob. "What's going on, Winger?"

When Holly looked at Bob, he was wiping his face with his handkerchief. "Nothing. I just brought over a pie. None of your concern, *Stanley*."

Bob's voice held a note of menace that Holly had never heard before. She edged closer to Stanley.

"Bob was just leaving," she said, noticing that the rain had almost stopped. "Tell your mother how much I appreciate the pie."

"Holly, I—"

Stanley stepped forward, his large frame towering over Bob. "Holly wants you to leave."

Bob stumbled down the steps and disappeared into the gray mist left by the rain.

Holly sagged against the porch column. "Stanley, thank you."

"What was going on?"

"Bob can get very upset."

"Are you all right?"

"I'm fine. But I need to go check on Uncle Virgil."

Stanley looked at his shoes, then back up at her. "Sure. Okay. The coaches sent over some soft drinks and stuff. I'll get them out of the car."

"Do you need some help?"

Stanley shook his head and smiled. "Nah. The head

coach's wife made a cake, but I can get everything in two trips.''

''Don't be silly. I'll get the cake,'' Holly said, following Stanley down the stairs.

Holly wished Jack would hurry home. She needed to let him know about Bob's bizarre actions. She couldn't wait to see him, to feel his comforting presence. If the DNA test on Donald Sheffield proved that he wasn't the killer, maybe Jack could force Bob to submit to DNA testing. Holly felt sure her nightmare was nearly over.

''The cake is in the back seat,'' Stanley said. ''Here, that door is tricky. I'll open it.''

When Stanley opened the door, Holly stepped around him to reach into the back seat, but Stanley grabbed her from behind.

''Sta—'' A soft cloth was pressed against her nose and mouth. Caught by surprise, it took her a second to react. She took a breath and realized there was some kind of chemical on the cloth.

She struggled, using all the techniques she had taught. She shoved her elbow backwards, tried to ram his nose with her head, kicked behind her at his groin—but he easily sidestepped each move. Then it occurred to her that Stanley had always been there in the gym whenever she taught a class. He had watched. He knew every move, so obviously he knew how to counter each one.

An icy terror took hold of her as she began to feel faint from holding her breath. She had to have air. Her lungs screaming, she finally gasped and got the full blast of the chemical. Her head reeled. She felt herself tumbling into the back seat of Stanley's old car.

Her last thought was that she would never see Jack again.

Chapter Thirteen

Jack cringed under Debi's horrified gaze. "So what you're saying is, you aren't really married? You're just pretending to be to try to catch a *stalker?*"

"We're married, but—" He spread his hands. "There's no time for this. I've got to find her. If he has her, then her life is in danger." Dread hung over him like a rock teetering on a precipice.

Debi's face was white as a sheet. "I went to take a shower as soon as I saw it was Bob Winger at the door. I couldn't face his whining. I thought maybe she'd gone somewhere with him."

Jack shook his head. "She wouldn't do that. She promised me she'd stay here. You're sure it was Winger?"

"Yes. There's a pie with Mrs. Winger's name on it by the door, and she doesn't drive." Debi scrutinized him. "So you don't know who's after my sister?"

"We were looking at Donald Sheffield, but he was pulling down a traffic ticket on his way to the casino boats in Vicksburg at the exact time the car tried to run us down." He looked at his watch, then checked his gun. "How long ago did you take your shower?"

"About twenty minutes. I thought she'd be back by

now.'' Debi clasped her hands together. ''Find her, Jack. Don't let anything happen to her.''

He clenched his jaw. What if he couldn't stop it? What if he was too late? He'd left her alone again, to go chasing after a dead end. If he'd stayed on Sheffield's lawyer, threatening jail time for violating his restraining order, he might have given up the traffic ticket as an alibi.

But Jack had been too eager to get back to Holly, to be beside her for her aunt's funeral. He'd let his emotions guide his actions, and now her safety was threatened. Hell, not just her safety, her life.

On the way to the Winger's house on Pecan Circle, his cell phone rang. It was Reese, a lab tech at the Quantico lab.

''Decker told me to call,'' he said. ''Seems there's no magnesium carbonate in the control sample from your parking lot.''

''Yeah? So what does that mean? Where did it come from?''

''There are several possibilities, but the most common use is for chalk. Gymnast's chalk.''

The gym. Jack thanked the lab tech as he jumped out of the car at Winger's house. Winger had been in the gym that night, right before the car nearly ran them down.

Jack banged on the door. When Mrs. Winger answered, he didn't take the time to be polite.

''FBI,'' he growled, flashing his badge and his gun. ''Where's your son?''

Mrs. Winger squeaked as he pushed past her. He checked the house, his gun at the ready, until he came to the last bedroom.

He banged on the door. ''Winger! FBI!''

After a few seconds the door opened. "What the—?"

Jack grabbed Bob Winger and flipped him, his forearm mashing the back of the smaller man's neck into the wall, his gun against Winger's cheek as his gaze briefly swept the small room. No indication of another person.

"Where is she?"

"Wha—?"

He pressed the gun's barrel into Winger's pasty skin. "Where—is—my—wife?" he ground out between clenched teeth, spooked more than he'd ever been in his life. He'd had some close calls with victims, but never had he felt so helpless, so defeated.

He'd failed Holly. She'd depended on him to keep her safe, and he hadn't.

And God help him if he was too late, because he didn't think he could live without her.

Bob whimpered, and Jack knew instinctively that he wasn't Holly's stalker. Frustrated and disgusted, he let Bob go, so fast the man crumpled to the floor.

"Get up." He resisted the urge to kick him. "Get up and tell me what happened."

Bob sat back flat on the floor and looked up at Jack with bloodshot, teary eyes. "I'm sorry," he sobbed. "I'm sorry. I shouldn't have gotten angry. I try so hard not to get angry anymore. I'm working on it."

Jack leveled his weapon at him. "Get—up."

Bob stared up the barrel of the gun and whimpered again, then scrambled to get his feet under him.

"What are you doing to Bobby?" Bob's mother squealed. "I'm going to call the police."

"Good," Jack snapped. "I'm going to need them."

As soon as Bob was standing, Jack backed him up
against the wall. "Talk to me."

Bob's face was bright red and smeared with tears.
"I yelled at her. Really scared her. She turned all
pale." He started sobbing. "I can't blame her. I
shouldn't—"

Jack jabbed him with his gun. "Facts."

Bob swallowed audibly. "Stanley Hanks came by.
He made me leave."

Hanks. The maintenance man from the university.
The guy who'd been in prison for five years…and who
worked every day at the gym.

Jack shoved Winger aside and ran out of the house.
He holstered his weapon and pulled out his cell phone
as he jumped into Holly's car. He dialed Virgil's number, but when he talked to Debi, she hadn't seen or
heard anything from Holly.

He sped toward Hanks' apartment, dialing Decker.
"Decker. Hanks is the killer. Get the locals down here.
I'm on my way to his house."

"They're on their way and so am I. Jack, hang back
and wait."

"Right." Jack disconnected. No way was he leaving
Holly alone with that madman any longer than he had
to. He had a horrific vision in his brain. Hanks had
taken things from Holly's house. He'd built a love
nest, a shrine to her purity. He'd waited for her to
come to him.

Jack's presence had fueled Hanks' obsession,
whipped it to a fever pitch, until his psychosis hadn't
allowed him to wait any longer. If Jack didn't find her
soon—

He stopped in front of Hanks' apartment. The maintenance man's car was nowhere in sight, but that didn't

stop Jack. He banged on the door, calling out to Hanks that he was a federal agent and to open up.

There was no response.

Jack kicked the door in. With his weapon gripped in both hands, he entered the apartment. Carefully he searched each room, examined each door, but the only thing out of the ordinary about Hanks' apartment was its very ordinariness. There were no dirty dishes, no magazines, no shirts or socks carelessly tossed aside. It was almost as if no one lived there.

Where were they? Where had Hanks taken all the things he'd stolen from Holly? Where had he furnished his love nest?

The gym. Of course.

Jumping back into his car and roaring away, Jack cursed the time he'd wasted at Hanks' apartment. The gym was Hanks' life. That's where he had watched and waited for Holly. Of course that's where he would build his secret love nest. There was certainly a secret storage space or subbasement that Hanks would know all about.

"Holly, hang on! I'm coming," he whispered, hoping he wasn't too late.

His brain refused to consider that possibility. He would find her. He had to find her. He couldn't live without her.

She was the bravest, kindest person he'd ever known. She'd taken the time to know him, really know him. She'd refused to allow him to lurk behind his wall of ice.

She'd shown him all he'd missed in his lonely life. Friends, family, the joy she derived from helping people. She'd shown him what it meant to love, and be loved.

Even if she couldn't forgive him for not telling her everything, even if she didn't love him like he loved her, he was a better person for having known her.

In front of the gym, Jack sat in his car for a precious second, blinking to clear the haze from his eyes. Grimly and deliberately, he forced his feelings back behind the wall. He needed cold logic, unimpaired by emotion, to save her. His love wouldn't help her. His expertise would.

He quickly assessed the building. There were only three outer doors—the main entrance, a fire door in the back of the gym, and an exit on one side.

Jack went to the main entrance. It was locked. He walked around and tried the other two doors. Both locked. The only windows were high, near the rounded roof. On the back of the gym was a slender metal fire-escape ladder. Holstering his gun, Jack started climbing.

STANLEY SAT at a cheap knockoff of a Victorian writing table, hunched over a notebook. He was dressed in dark pants and a flowing white shirt with ruffled sleeves. He wrote furiously, mumbling to himself.

Holly watched him in horrified fascination from her position on a beautiful lace-draped brass bed as she tried to ease the pain in her arms, which were pulled over her head and tied to the headboard.

She was confused and drowsy. Where were they? What had happened? And why was Stanley dressed like a pirate, or a poet? She tried to remember. She'd reached into the car for the cake and the next thing she knew she was overcome by some chemical, maybe chloroform?

She vaguely remembered Stanley leading her down

here, helping her walk, half carrying her. Jack would be so disappointed. She should have done a better job of defending herself. She should have escaped. But Stanley was so strong. Her arms and shins were bruised and aching from her efforts.

He'd forced her down the metal stairs to a large and well-furnished room. There he'd given her a choice. She could change into what he called her "virginal nightdress" or he would do it for her. She'd complied. Then he'd grabbed her arms and placed that cloth over her nose and mouth again.

The sound of a heavy object hitting the floor above her head had woken her. She'd found herself alone, lying on the bed with her arms tied above her head and her bare feet tied together. But the drug was still in her system and she hadn't been able to keep her eyes open.

Later—how much later she did not know—Stanley had reappeared in the room.

"Stanley, please talk to me."

She'd been trying to get him to talk to her, but he'd been engrossed in whatever he was writing, and hadn't even looked up.

"Stanley, you're scaring me." She tugged on the soft cloths that bound her hands. Did she feel something give, or was it just wishful thinking?

She looked around. The room was furnished with odd bits of furniture. Aside from the brass bed with its single, hard mattress and the imitation Victorian desk, there were a couple of metal folding chairs, several plastic exercise steps stacked beside the bed, and an old floor lamp. It must have taken him hours, days even, to get these pieces down here to the secret chamber he'd created.

Love nest. Jack's words came back to her with ominous meaning. Stanley had spent years preparing this underground room. Did people even know there was a room down here?

How would Jack ever find them? A horrible thought came to her. She didn't know how long she'd lain here unconscious. Was Jack all right?

She stared at Stanley, looking for the killer beneath his quiet, bland exterior. She still couldn't believe it.

"'Outside are the storms and strangers: we, oh, close, safe, warm sleep I and she—I and she'!" His voice was soft, his face tranquil. He glanced up at her and indicated the leather-bound book. "See? I write to you every morning. It's my promise to you. The first thing I do when I wake."

He was talking oddly too, not just his words, but his tone, his inflection. He'd always been plain, hard-working Stanley. Now he had transformed into someone she didn't know.

He pointed at the bookshelf over the desk, on which sat at least ten books identical to the one he held.

Holly stared dumbstruck at the journals as Stanley continued to talk.

"Each journal represents a year. You will read them all, my dear. They hold our history, everything we have done to be together."

He was crazy. Ten years of journals. He'd been watching her all that time. At least they would prove that he was the killer, if what he wrote was comprehensible.

Holly had been afraid before, but terror seized her limbs now, sending spasms through them. Even her lungs and heart cramped within her until she could hardly breathe. Stanley, who had worked beside her in the gym for hours, who had walked her to her car many a night after her aerobics students had left, who had come to Brad's funeral, and Danny's.

This quiet man she'd gone to high school with had entered her house and touched her things. He had snuffed out three precious lives in his obsessive madness.

The various items she had misplaced over the years were displayed with eerie care around the room, along with newspaper clippings and photos of her. Her engagement picture. A photo from a charity event she'd organized. But some were candid snapshots taken with an instant camera. He'd followed her, taken pictures of her, in her car, running in the mornings, through the open blinds in her living room. She shuddered in revulsion.

Her wedding dress hung beside the desk. Her stuffed bear from childhood, with Brad's class ring around its neck, and her makeup kit sat on the desk, along with her mother's cup. A couple of pillows from her house adorned the bed, and, of course, she wore the white revealing gown that had disappeared from her lingerie drawer.

Jack had been right. His profile of her stalker as a loner, near her age, an underachiever in an undemanding job fit Stanley perfectly.

Oh God, Jack. Where are you? How long had she been here? Surely by now Jack had gotten back from Jackson and found out that Bob had come to the house.

He'd probably tracked Bob down and found out she'd left with Stanley. Would Jack think to check the gym? She hoped he'd see Stanley's car, parked near the back entrance.

Stanley put away his pen and closed his notebook.

"Now. I've written my daily letter to you, my little Portuguese." His eyes glittered as his gaze swept over her, from her bound hands all the way to her toes. He picked up an ornate letter opener and toyed with it.

She stared at him. "But I'm here," she said cautiously, wondering what he was planning to do to her, wondering if there was anything she could say that would appease him.

"You don't need to write to me. You can talk to me now. Tell me what you want, Stanley."

"Ah, Holly. I want for nothing now. 'Thy soul's mine: and thus, grown perfect. Life will just hold out the proving, Both our powers, alone and blended: And then, come next life quickly! This world's use will have been ended.'"

Listening to his words, Holly grew chill with fear. He was going to kill her and himself. *'This world's use will have been ended.'*

"You see what I have done for us. We can finally be together forever, as we promised each other all those years ago."

Holly frowned. *Promised?* What was he taking about? "Our promise," she repeated. Maybe if she played along, she could gain some understanding of why he'd targeted her.

"Oh, tell mc again." She hoped he hadn't heard her voice quaver. "I love to hear you tell it." She tried to swallow but her mouth was dry with terror.

"We sat together and chose the perfect poems. We must have two, you said, and the teacher agreed. "Love in a Life" and "Life in a Love." We practiced until we knew the words by heart, those beautiful words Robert Browning wrote for his wife. That's when it began. We couldn't reveal our love. Ah, Holly.

'How sad and bad and mad it was— But then, how it was sweet!'

Holly stared in horrified fascination at the man whom she had known since high school.

English class, senior year.

She had a vague recollection of meeting him a couple of times after school to practice their presentation. The whole class had been paired up for poetry readings.

So that was it. That's when this all began. Bile rose in her throat, making her nauseated. *Oh God, Jack, please hurry.*

"But, Stanley, Brad and I went steady all through high school. You were his friend. He asked you to take me to the senior prom when he couldn't because of his injured ankle."

"Yes. Yes." Stanley's eyes grew brighter. He set the book aside and touched Holly's cheek. She tried not to cringe away from him. "You remember. We knew even then that we were meant to be together."

Her clearest memory was of Stanley backing her against a table at the dance, trying to kiss her. She'd said no, just as one of Brad's football buddies had come upon them.

"Brad tried to get rid of me by forcing me to go to prison, but our love survived even that."

Stanley was mad. He'd rewritten history to match his madness. "You went to prison for using your father's gun to rob a liquor store," she said.

"That's what Brad told everyone."

He stood and paced, twirling the silver, rapier-shaped letter opener between his fingers, his eyes following the glint of light off the sharpened blade. Holly tried to focus on him, rather than on the shiny metal.

"Stanley, what are you going to do?"

He whirled and grabbed her hair. "You are my love. Mine. If we die together, then so be it, for death and life are one and the same."

Holly winced as he pulled on her hair and brandished the letter opener, but he only cut one strand and curled it around his fingers. He looked at it and spoke under his breath. "'I shall hear her knock in the worst of a storm's uproar, I shall pull her through the door, I shall have her for evermore'!"

Jack, where are you? Holly cried silently.

JACK TURNED THE KNOB of the door to the men's locker room. It felt slick and greasy. His heart jumped. Damn. He looked at his hand, which was smeared with a light oily liquid. He rubbed his fingers together, then sniffed.

A jolt of adrenaline shot through him. The substance was clear and odorless, but he knew with a growing dread that it probably contained a lethal poison. He should have used gloves. He quickly wiped the residue on his slacks, knowing he had to get to a sink to wash his hands as quickly as possible.

Although, if the oily substance was dimethyl sulfoxone, it was probably already too late.

Dimethyl sulfoxone, or DMSO, was a unique chemical. He'd learned about it as part of his FBI training. It was absorbed into the body through the skin, and anything dissolved in it was also absorbed. Athletes sometimes used it as a liniment for aches and pains, but it had been used by assassins too, to deliver poison in a nearly undetectable manner.

He stood back and kicked the door. It gave easily, and as he stumbled forward, a fifty-pound weight glanced off one shoulder and another hit his back. He fell, biting back a shout at the pain, then rolled and regained his feet.

He ran to the nearest sink and scrubbed his hands, hoping the soap and water would slow the action of whatever poison Hanks had used.

Moving quickly and efficiently, he took two small envelopes out of his pocket. Using a torn piece of the first envelope, he rubbed it on the knob, then dropped it into the second envelope and sealed it, jotting the time, date, place and his suspicions on the front. He stuck it back into his pocket. He wanted a record of what he'd touched and where, in case he wasn't around to talk about it in person.

It occurred to him that he might already be dying. He'd never worried about that before. His job had always been his life, and if he died protecting an innocent, then so be it.

But suddenly, desperately, he wanted to live. He had to rescue Holly. His heart pounded hard against his chest wall, and he wasn't sure if it was the poison or the fear that he would be too late to save Holly.

Glancing around quickly, he saw there were only two doors in the men's locker room—the door to the showers and the door to the linen closet.

He looked at the closet. It was big, a walk-in with shelves across the back. As Jack grabbed a towel to dry his hands he scrutinized the walls. Was that panel on the right wall out of alignment?

He pushed. The panel gave. It was a door. A piece of torn cloth hanging from a nail served as the knob.

Jack carefully slid the door open and shone his high-powered pocket flashlight into the blackness. There were metal stairs leading downward.

His pulse raced. This was where Hanks had taken Holly. He was sure of it.

A taste like garlic filled his mouth and certainty settled like rocks in his gut. The characteristic taste of DMSO in his saliva meant the chemical was already entering his bloodstream, along with whatever poison Hanks had combined with it.

As if on cue, his hand started to burn.

He pulled out his cell phone and dialed Decker.

"Mitch." He could hear the rhythmic beat of helicopter blades through the phone line. Decker was on his way. He prayed his boss would arrive in time to save Holly.

"Jack. Where the hell are you?"

"He's got her in the subbasement of the gym. He knows I'm here."

"There are three field agents on their way, along with Detective Polk. You wait for them."

"Can't." Jack's chest was becoming tight. His hands and feet were tingling. It was getting hard to breathe. "No time. Listen. Have the…lab check Danny's body—" His breathing was becoming short. "DMSO. Check…hands, feet."

"That's how he was poisoned? How do you know?"

"Gotta go, Decker."

"Jack!"

"Tell T-Bone…door in the linen closet. Men's locker room. Hurry. And call an ambulance. I think I may be going into anaphylactic shock."

Jack heard Decker's shout but he didn't have time to explain. He thrust the cell phone back into his pocket without turning it off. Decker could listen in.

He licked his dry lips, noticing that his tongue already felt swollen.

He'd never gone in much for praying, but he prayed now—for the strength to get to Holly, to see her one more time, to save her from Hanks. He prayed for the courage to tell her how much he loved her, how in three days she'd changed his life forever.

He stepped into the blackness.

HOLLY HEARD THE HEAVY THUDS above their heads. Hope pumped through her veins like adrenaline. Was it Jack?

Stanley turned from replacing the textbook. He made a sweeping gesture toward the ceiling of the tiny room, his ruffled sleeve waving. "Listen, my love. It is your lover. He has found us."

Her heart pounded in her breast. Jack was here. All she had to do was keep Stanley focused on her, to give Jack a chance to sneak up on him.

"You think he will rescue you. So fickle. You have yet to learn that I am the only one who is true." Stanley turned a page in the book. "Worry not about your husband. If he did not succumb to the heavy weights that felled him, he will soon feel the wasp's sting."

Holly jerked in shock. Dread tasted like gall in her mouth. "Wasp's sting?"

Stanley cocked his head and glanced up. "Right now, your defiler is either dead from the weights that crushed his head, or dying from the wasp venom that swirls in his veins. Either way, he is doomed and you are mine."

"Why are you doing this?" Holly shouted in frustration, jerking on her bonds. She felt some give in the knot that tied her hands to the brass headboard. A thrill of hope raced through her with such ferocity that she almost cried out.

Her arms ached, but she couldn't afford to let them relax now. If the knot was coming loose, she had to hide that fact from Stanley until she could get the drop on him.

He was so strong, though, and her arms hurt so badly.

"Why? Because you are mine, my love. I waited so long for you to come to me. I carefully eliminated those who turned your head and I waited. Now there is only one last barrier to our love." He gestured again.

How had Stanley lived for so long in this small town without anyone realizing he was insane? He'd always been quiet, kept to himself, never said much. He'd been practically invisible. She could hear Jack's voice echoing in her head. *Classic serial-killer profile.*

Now he was going to kill Jack. She didn't understand everything he'd said, but she believed his vow to eliminate the last barrier. And she knew that last barrier was Jack.

"Stanley, please don't hurt him. I'll do what you want, I promise." Her pulse beat frantically in her throat. She needed to get loose, to somehow immobilize Stanley until Jack got here.

Stanley stood and paced. "Don't you see? It's too late now. You did not come to me. We could have been so happy. We could have lived together, and chased each other through the house, and slept together and written in our journals together. But you wasted your time and your love on those unworthy of you, and now, all that's left for us is the ultimate. We must die together."

He stopped and listened. ''I must go see if your husband has succumbed to my efforts.''

''Wait!'' Holly looked around frantically, searching for something to distract Stanley long enough for Jack to find them. Carefully she pulled on the strips of cloth. They gave a bit more as Stanley turned to look at her.

''What is it now, my treacherous love?'' he asked.

Her gaze lit on her wedding gown. ''Let me wear my wedding gown for you,'' she said, her voice quavering. She swallowed hard and fought for control. ''If we must die together, let us die as bride and groom.'' She watched him carefully. She didn't remember much of Browning, and she wasn't very poetically inclined, but maybe she could entice him with her pitiful efforts.

His pale blue eyes narrowed on her, and for a moment she was afraid he'd seen through her ruse. But then he turned and looked at the dress.

''Bride and groom,'' he said thoughtfully, then turned back to her. ''I like you better in your virginal gown, but it cannot restore your purity. I saw you and your faithless lover entwined. I saw you betray me. I waited patiently, but you liked their defilement, didn't you. You wanted it.''

Holly could see the whites around his eyes. He was raving.

''Perhaps…'' he whispered, looking back at the gown hanging beside the desk. ''Perhaps it would be fitting. You dying as a bride, with I your true groom.'' He reached to pull down the dress.

With a fierce tug, Holly pulled the knot on her bindings loose. The muscles in her arms cramped with pain, but she bit her lip and pushed through the agony. She grabbed the ends of the cloth that had tied her wrists to the headboard. In a swift, jerky movement, she pulled her bound feet under her and lunged at Stanley, throwing the strip of cloth over his head and crossing her wrists, tightening the impromptu garrote around his throat.

He yelped and shoved himself backward, falling on top of her on the bed, knocking her crown against the headboard.

As she fought to clear her blurred vision, a crash sounded at the door to the little room and she saw Jack, bathed in all the stars that were bursting in front of her eyes.

Jack looked like an angel. A wavering angel, holding himself up by sheer force of will, his left hand gripping the door facing, his face marred by red patches and his breathing rasping loudly in the quiet room.

"Get off her, Hanks," he croaked, leveling his gun at Stanley, who was still on top of her.

Struggling to pull air into her lungs, Holly tugged on the cloth she'd wrapped around Stanley's throat, but he got his fingers around it and thrust it over his head, jerking her bound wrists.

"Go ahead, O'Hara. Shoot. My true love and I wish to die together, anyway."

Jack struggled for one more breath. His throat was fast closing up. His lungs weren't working right, and he could barely see. He knew if he tried to shoot Hanks he might hit Holly. But he didn't have long, and if he didn't do something, Holly would definitely die.

His hand was burning like fire and his fingers would hardly move, but he squeezed the trigger.

Hanks cried out and lunged at him, knocking him backward. The man was quick and strong. Knowing he didn't have much time before the full force of the wasp venom kicked in, Jack tried to get off another shot, but his fingers wouldn't work—he was losing motor control.

He saw Holly moving. "Holly, get out of here," he shouted, hearing his voice come out choked and hoarse. "Go get help."

But as Hanks lunged at him, Holly, with strips of cloth dangling from her wrists, appeared behind him and stabbed him with something. Hanks screeched and arched backward, knocking Holly down, then lunged again at Jack.

Jack wrapped his hand around his gun, concentrating on making his hand work. He endured the force of Hanks' head butting him in the stomach, and went with the blow.

He felt he was moving in slow motion as he stuck the barrel in Hanks' ribs and pulled the trigger.

Chapter Fourteen

Holly paced back and forth in the Intensive Care waiting room. After she'd been examined and released, Debi had brought her some clothes. Holly's brain was still hazy from the effects of the chloroform, but she had refused to leave the hospital until Jack's condition could be determined.

The paramedics who'd rushed Jack to the hospital had explained how he'd been poisoned. Holly had heard of DMSO but she'd never seen it used. In the ambulance, Jack had been intubated to help him breathe, and then, before they could get to Forrest General, he'd convulsed, his body writhing in a violent seizure, and the EMTs had pushed her aside to administer more epinephrine.

Jack had been rushed straight into the Intensive Care Unit to receive life support while physicians assessed the damage wrought by the wasp venom and the anaphylactic reaction on his system.

So Holly waited. As a physical therapist, she'd worked in and around hospitals her whole career, but today she felt helpless and lost.

Please, God, don't let him die, she prayed silently.

I can make myself go on without him in my life if I have to, but I can't live knowing he died to save me.

A hand touched her shoulder.

"Holly?" an unfamiliar voice said.

She turned to face a tall, powerful man with kind eyes and wind-tousled hair.

"I'm Mitchell Decker."

"Special Agent Decker."

His eyes crinkled at the corners. "Call me Mitch." He took her hand. "I understand he's still sedated."

She nodded, tears clogging her throat. "I haven't seen him. They took him straight into ICU. He went into anaphylactic shock. Stanley poisoned him—" She couldn't continue.

Mitch put his arm around Holly's shoulders. "I know," he said quietly. "Jack called me on his cell phone. He figured out that was how Hanks killed Danny. Hanks must have entered Danny's apartment after he'd fallen unconscious from the poison and stuck a wasp stinger in his neck, then removed whatever object he'd coated with the venom and planted in the apartment.

"As soon as Jack realized that Hanks had coated the doorknob in the gym with poison, he preserved a sample in an evidence envelope, labeled it with all the necessary information and put it in his jacket pocket."

Holly laughed, a little hiccuping sound. "He never gives up, does he."

"That's how the Ice Man is."

She wiped her eyes and looked up at him. "Ice Man?"

Mitch's clear blue eyes went round. "He didn't tell you his nickname?"

She shook her head. "No, but I can see why people might think of him that way."

"People who don't know him."

Holly smiled and nodded. "People who don't know him," she agreed. Then she sobered. "Do you know if Stanley made it?" She couldn't believe she had actually stabbed him with his letter opener. But he had been attacking Jack, and she'd had to do something to stop him.

"Hanks is upstairs in surgery. Your stab wound punctured his lung, and Jack's second shot hit a rib and glanced off his side. He'll live to stand trial."

"Thank God I didn't kill him," she breathed. "Although, for a minute there…"

Decker patted her hand.

A doctor came into the waiting room, and the sight of him sheared Holly's breath. But he stepped over to another family. "Oh God, I can't stand this. I need to see him."

"Let me see if I can use my influence." Mitch disappeared.

About twenty minutes later, he returned, took her hand and sat down with her in the corner of the waiting room. The terror that had grabbed hold of her when she'd first realized what Stanley had done now squeezed her insides. She could barely speak.

"What's wrong?" she whispered, not wanting to know the answer.

"Jack is very sick. His body is fighting off the effects of the venom, but he may be going into renal failure. We're helicoptering a specialist down from Jackson. And as soon as he can be moved, I'm taking him back to D.C."

Holly's eyes brimmed over with tears. Just as she'd

known from the beginning, Jack would finish his job and leave. He had a life, a career that had nothing to do with her. She was just an assignment, although she could have sworn at times that she meant more to him than that.

But the most important thing was that he was all right. "He'll be alive, won't he?" Her breath caught in a little sob. "Can I see him?"

Mitch's soft blue gaze held hers. "I'm not sure you should right now. He's intubated. He's going to look pretty bad, and he can't talk."

Tears flowed down Holly's cheeks. "I just need to see him for a minute. I just need to—" She paused.

Mitch waited.

"Touch him." More tears spilled over.

"Come on."

Mitch took her through the ICU doors and into a room on the left. There was a nurse fiddling with an IV pump, but Holly saw no one but Jack.

He was intubated, and a ventilator helped him breathe. His right hand had an IV line in it. His chest was bare, the scars on his shoulders bright red.

She studied his face. His eyes were closed, lashes resting against his hollowed cheeks. His face and neck still bore a few spots of red.

She touched his hand. "Oh, Jack."

His fingers twitched but he didn't open his eyes.

"He's asleep, Mrs. O'Hara," the nurse said on her way out of the room. "He probably won't know you're here. He might be more alert the next time you come in."

Holly leaned over and kissed Jack's stubbled cheek.

"I'll wait outside," Mitch said.

She pushed Jack's hair back from his forehead and

smoothed the corner of a piece of tape on his hand. He looked thin and vulnerable in the white hospital bed. And his face was so pale.

"Jack, the nurse said you don't know I'm here. That's probably good, because I have to say something to you, and I'm not real sure I could say it if those icy gray eyes were staring at me." She smiled through tears.

"Thank you, Jack O'Hara. Thank you for making me feel safe and protected. Thank you for making me feel like I was the most important thing in your life. Thank you for treating me like an equal, and not letting me feel sorry for myself. Thank you for sharing a part of your life with me that I don't think you usually share."

She sobbed and clamped a hand over her mouth. "I swore I was not going to...cry." She wiped her eyes. "And I'm not."

Sitting up straight, she caressed his forearm above the IV site. "I know you're very sick, but I also know you never give up. So I know you won't give up this time, either. Special Agent Decker is going to take you back to Washington so he can take care of you.

"If I know you, you'll be back on the job in no time. Save as many of them as you can, Jack. It's what you do best. And thank you for saving me."

A nurse tapped on the glass door of the room.

Holly looked up and nodded. "I have to go now, but I'll be back during the next visit schedule. I'll be here as long as you are."

She stood, then leaned over and kissed his cheek gently. "I love you, Jack O'Hara." She wiped her tear off his cheek, then left.

EVEN BEFORE THE GRUMPY evening-shift nurse informed him, Jack knew he wasn't being a good boy. He was sick of the hospital, sick of the tests and sick of the nurses that came around every fifteen minutes to check his vitals.

He knew he should be grateful and appreciative, and he was. But he wasn't sick anymore. He needed to get out of here. Decker had informed him that he was taking Jack back to D.C. this morning. Jack had protested, but Decker was firm.

"It's not like I'm injured," Jack had insisted.

Decker had given him his patient look. "No, it's not like you almost went into renal failure and died."

"That's just it. *I didn't.*"

But Decker had won the argument by default, because an orderly had come in to wheel Jack downstairs for some final tests.

Now he was pacing his room, waiting for the doctor to write discharge orders and contemplating leaving the hospital AMA—against medical advice.

Someone knocked on the door.

"Come in," Jack barked, "especially if you have my discharge orders."

Holly walked in, bringing all the sunshine in the South with her. Jack's heart did a flip and he couldn't help but smile. She had on a bright yellow dress that emphasized her delicate curves and left her sleek legs bare.

"Hi," she said, smiling at him.

He studied her face. Was that sadness back? "Are you okay?"

She pressed her lips together for an instant, then smiled even wider. "Of course I am, thanks to you."

He couldn't take his eyes off her. She was so beau-

tiful it made his heart hurt. He could see evidence of
bruises on her forearms and wrists. Each one was a
testament to her bravery and strength. He'd love to
hold her close and kiss away the pain.

He lifted his gaze back to hers and felt the arc of
fire that jolted him each time their eyes met. He held
out his arms.

She came right to him, wrapped her arms around his
waist and put her head against his chest. He breathed
in the strawberry scent of her hair.

"Look at you," she said, her voice strained.
"You're all dressed and ready to go. The last time I
saw you, you were still groggy."

He pushed her away so he could look at her.
"That's right. Where have you been the past twenty
hours since you visited me?"

Her eyes grew wide. Did it surprise her that he knew
exactly how long it had been since he'd last seen her?

"Today was my first day back at work. It was a
really busy day. I just came from the Rehab Center."
She looked away, out the window, then back at him.
"I wanted to see you before you left."

Jack felt a strange sensation. He recognized it. He
even remembered the last time he'd felt it. It had been
a long time ago, when he was just thirteen years old.
It was the feeling of tears burning the backs of his
eyes. He cleared his throat.

"So I just wanted to say goodbye, and thank you,"
she said, smiling brightly again, although he thought
he could see a suspicious mistiness in her eyes.

"Holly…"

"When will Special Agent Decker be here?"

She was making this so hard. He assessed her. Was
she trying to let him down easily, give him the ability

to say goodbye without any embarrassing revelations? He'd heard her whisper "I love you" in his ear while he was intubated and too weak to open his eyes. Was that just the grateful emotion of a victim whose life he'd saved?

It was too late to worry about that. He had some things to say and he was determined to say them.

"Holly, I'm so sorry."

"What?" She stared at him in surprise. "Sorry for what? You *saved* me. You could have died, and yet you found me and you fought him and you saved me. There's nothing in this world for you to be sorry for."

He shook his head and took a ragged breath. "I didn't mean to—"

She put her fingers against his mouth. "Please don't, Jack. Not yet."

He took her hand in his. "Holly. I need to tell you something. It's important." And he had no idea how he was going to do it. How did a man who had never allowed himself to love anyone say "I love you"? How did a man who had lived his life alone ask a woman to live the rest of her life with him?

And how would he live if she didn't feel the same way?

"I've never had much of a family. Always liked living alone. Liked doing my job, then stepping away." He stopped.

Holly listened to Jack's halting words and had the urge to put her hands over her ears. She wanted to reach out and take hold of his heart and force him to love her as much as she loved him. She wanted to beg him not to walk away this time, but she didn't have the courage. He walked away. That's who he was.

"I made mistakes. Mistakes that almost got you killed. I didn't mean to get involved."

His words pierced her wounded heart. "Oh, don't, Jack." *Don't go back behind that icy barrier.* Tears spilled down her cheeks.

"I didn't mean to fall in love with you."

She couldn't move.

"You...what?" Had she heard him right? Hope swelled inside her like the sun rising to brighten a new day. It crept into the dark corners of her heart and pushed out the fear, banished the loneliness.

He tugged on her hand and lay it against his chest, against his heart. "Feel that?"

She nodded, unable to speak. She spread her hand over his chest and felt the steady, strong beat.

"That's my heart. Unfrozen. Because of you."

Her own heart soared. Shock and happiness stole her breath. All she could do, it seemed, was cry.

"You made me want to open up." His gray eyes glittered like silver as he watched her warily. "You slipped inside me, where no one had ever bothered to go. You healed me."

He reached up, caught a tear on his thumb and looked at it.

"I've wanted to do that ever since I met you," he whispered.

"Do what?"

"Stop your tears."

She cradled his beautiful face in her hands and kissed him. "Oh, Jack. When did you get to be such a romantic?"

He laughed and pressed kisses along the line of her jaw. "Will you run away with me and love me forever?" he murmured.

"I can't," she said, laughing. "I'm a married woman."

"That's okay. I'm a married man."

Holly kissed the rough stubble on his cheek. "I love you, Jack O'Hara."

He smiled down at her. "I know you do. I heard you the first time."

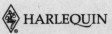

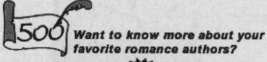

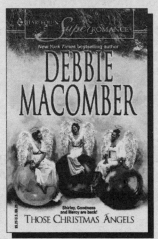

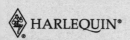
HARLEQUIN®

INTRIGUE®

Nestled deep in the Cascade Mountains of Oregon, the close-knit community of Timber Falls is visited by evil. Could one of their own be lurking in the shadows…?

CASCADES CONCEALED

B.J. Daniels

takes you on a journey to the remote Northwest in a new series of books far removed from the fancy big city. Here, folks are down-to-earth, but some have a tendency toward trouble when the rainy season comes…and it's about to start pouring!

Look for

MOUNTAIN SHERIFF
December 2003

and

DAY OF RECKONING
March 2004

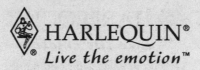

HARLEQUIN®
Live the emotion™

Visit us at www.eHarlequin.com

HICQMS

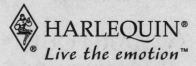